'You're very good with children,'

Mandy told him as he held her youngest.

Lucas didn't want to be good with children. He didn't want to be anything except what he was—a man who travelled light and travelled alone.

But Mandy was watching him with a face that shone as if she'd scrubbed it with moonbeams. And Lucas could do nothing but smile.

The air was soft, the child in his arms cuddly and the woman beside him sweet smelling.

A long stretch of lonely years trailed behind him.

And for one dangerous, outrageous moment, Lucas Gray Wolf, arch loner, ached for what might have been…

Dear Reader,

A warm welcome to Special Edition.

Considering Kate, a new STANISLASKI novel by number one *New York Times* bestselling author Nora Roberts, is our first book this month and also available from mid-July is the linked book, *The Stanislaski Sisters*, which contains Kate's mother's story.

Our popular THAT'S MY BABY! mini-series continues with *My Little One* by Linda Randall Wisdom. See how this marriage-of-convenience-for-the-sake-of-the-baby story turns out. Talking of children, look out for the first book in a new trilogy from wonderful author Laurie Paige. *Something To Talk About* begins THE WINDRAVEN LEGACY where newly-discovered secrets threaten to shatter the lives and loves of this family. The second book, *When I See Your Face*, is out in July.

The third of the MONTANA BRIDES linked books—*Just Pretending* by Myrna Mackenzie—storms onto the shelves this month. Along with five orphaned children, including nine-month-old triplets, in *Mother in a Moment* by Allison Leigh and a passionate lone wolf in *Gray Wolf's Woman* by Peggy Webb.

Enjoy!

The Editors

Gray Wolf's Woman

PEGGY WEBB

™ SILHOUETTE®

SPECIAL EDITION™

*Silhouette, Silhouette Special Edition and Colophon are
registered trademarks of Harlequin Books S.A., used under licence.*

*First published in Great Britain 2002
Silhouette Books, Eton House, 18-24 Paradise Road,
Richmond, Surrey TW9 1SR*

© Peggy Webb 2000

ISBN 0 373 24347 2

23-0602

*Printed and bound in Spain
by Litografia Rosés S.A., Barcelona*

and her two chocolate labs live in a hundred-year-old house not far from the farm where she grew up. 'A farm is a wonderful place for dreaming,' she says. 'I used to sit in the hayloft and dream of being a writer.' Now, with two grown children and more than forty-five romance novels to her credit, the former English teacher confesses she's still a hopeless romantic and loves to create the happy endings her readers love so well.

When she isn't writing, she can be found at her piano playing blues and jazz or in one of her gardens planting flowers. A believer in the idea that a person should never stand still, Peggy recently taught herself carpentry.

Acknowledgements:

No book is ever written in a vacuum.
For *Gray Wolf's Woman* I owe special thanks to
Dr Bill Rice and Lou Remmers, PT, for putting my
broken wrist back in shape to type, to my family
and friends who surround me with a bulwark of love,
encouragement and emotional support, and to
Tom Wesson Jr for caving info and the incredible
experience of biking. Hugs to all of you.
As always, I claim responsibility for any mistakes I've
made in the portrayal of things beyond my ken.

Prologue

When Mandy first saw the man in the woods, she thought she must be hallucinating. She'd heard that stress sometimes would do that to a person.

If he *was* a hallucination, he was the most dangerous one she'd ever had. The man was completely swathed in black, his face hidden behind the visor of a crash helmet, and he was roaring toward her on one of those big expensive motorcycles that sound like Judgment Day is coming. He might have been the very devil himself, and yet the sight of him sent Mandy completely awhirl.

He was a big man, and even across all that space he exuded protectiveness, as if he were somebody she'd want to run to if she needed to climb onto a lap, and at the same time, someone who'd light every one of her fires if she did.

She figured she must be going stark raving crazy, which didn't surprise her, considering the circumstances.

A woman whose son was lost was bound to imagine rescue on every corner.

Shifting Jill on her hip, she turned to her other daughter.

"Do you see what I see, Betsy?"

"It's a man, Mommy. A big one. And he's got somebody with him."

The news did nothing to relieve Mandy's anxiety. The last thing she needed right now was an encounter with a dangerous stranger *and* his cohort in the deep woods. Even if she screamed there'd be nobody around to hear.

She eased her daughters behind the shelter of a bush. "Stay down, now, and keep quiet."

The roar became louder, and as the motorcycle came closer, Mandy saw that the person behind the driver was a small boy wearing a helmet too large for his head and bright-red high-top sneakers, one tied with neon-green string. Betsy saw him at the same time.

"Look, Mommy. It's Rusty," she said.

"Stay here," she commanded.

Then Mandy picked up the biggest stick she could find and stepped out to face the man who had kidnapped her son.

Chapter One

There was nothing like roaring down the open road on a motorcycle to make a man feel good. With nine hundred pounds of power between his legs and a belly full of the fish he'd caught in the Tennessee River, Lucas Gray Wolf was on top of the world. He had a bedroll, a fishing pole and a trusty GoldWing motorcycle, and his best friend and partner Steve Thunderhorse was taking care of the ranch back in Arizona.

What more could a man want?

Twice a year he set out on his bike, going wherever whim took him. This year whim and some good back roads had led him all the way to Pickwick where Mississippi, Alabama and Tennessee converged at the Tennessee River. Quite a change from the stark, red buttes and wide-open spaces of Paradise Ranch.

Still, Lucas liked what he saw. He liked the gentle

rolling hills, the lush greenery, the river that meandered in a fashion suited to the slow pace of the Deep South.

Spotting an eagle in the distance riding the air currents, Lucas eased his bike down to a sedate pace and blazed a trail through the woods. He parked under the shade of a giant oak tree, peeled off his black jumpsuit and helmet, then hiked in the direction he'd spotted the eagle.

As Lucas made his way around a tangle of wild berry brambles, he heard a sound that didn't belong in the woods, a muffled cry coming from the west. Moving with the silent grace of his Sioux ancestors, Lucas set off in that direction.

"Help. Somebody help me." The cries came from underground, the voice of a child, probably scared to death.

"Where are you?" Lucas shouted.

"Down in this hole. Are you going to talk all day, or are you coming to get me out?"

Lucas grinned. Scratch "scared." This kid was spunky. "Keep talking so I can locate you." The kid started whistling "Dixie." Within minutes Lucas was atop a ridge looking down into the mouth of a cave.

"Are you hurt?"

"Naw, I ain't hurt. I'm madder'n a hornet."

"I'll have you out of there in a little while, but first I have to go back to my bike and get some rope."

The kid's parents must be frantic. As he raced back to his motorcycle, Lucas scanned the woods for signs of life—another human being, a campsite, the ashes from a dead campfire. As far as the eye could see, there was nothing except ridges and trees and the ribbon of water that sparkled in the glare of a burning summer sun.

Lucas traveled light, partially because he had only a small storage space on the back of the bike, but mostly because that's the way he liked it. He always carried supplies for emergencies, though—rope, first-aid kit, hunting knife, flashlight, and plenty of Snickers chocolate bars.

In his forty years, Lucas had done just about everything a man craving adventure could want to do—skydiving, mountain climbing, paragliding, spelunking. If there was a risk to be taken, he took it.

In his caving days, he'd carried rappeling equipment in an extra backpack when he hit the road, in case he came across a cave that hadn't been ruined by tourists and commercialism. He used to believe he would discover a cave. The thrill of rappeling down into a black hole, where no one had ever been before, used to keep him awake at night.

That had never happened, of course. Caving had been ruined by people. Most human beings had no respect for the land. Some even had the audacity to believe it belonged to them. Lucas knew better. His name was on the deed to Paradise Ranch, but he never fooled himself into believing he owned the land. He was merely a caretaker for the next generation. He treated the land with the same respect and reverence that his Sioux ancestors had.

All was quiet back at the cave. Lucas knelt to shine the flashlight into the opening. "I'm back, kid." There was no answer. "Are you all right down there?"

"I had to take a leak. There's something dead back there. It stinks like hell."

Lucas grinned. Maybe this kid was an orphan. Lucas remembered what it was like when he'd been small and scared and alone in the world. He had peppered his language with every bad word he'd ever heard and some he'd made up on the spot just to show everybody that he wasn't scared of anything.

"I'm going to anchor this rope, then come down to get you. It may take a while, so be patient."

"Hell, mister, patience is my middle name."

Lucas laughed. "What's the rest of your name?"

There was a long silence as if the kid were deciding how much to tell a stranger.

"My name's Rusty and that's all I'm telling." His voice was so belligerent he might as well have added, Do you want to make something of it? "What's yours?"

"Lucas Gray Wolf." With a half hitch he secured the rope around a tree, then eased himself over the lip of the opening and began to rappel down the limestone walls.

"You made that up."

"No, I didn't. Gray Wolf is my name. My father was Sioux."

"Sue? That's a girl's name."

"Sioux as in Native American."

"Wow."

Lucas shone his flashlight on his surroundings. The walls were ridged, so the boy had probably had some precarious holds going down. Near the bottom those petered out, and the walls became so sheer that coming back up the same way would be impossible. Finally, Lucas spotted the boy. He could just make out the top of Rusty's head.

"I'm almost there, Rusty."

"I got eyes. I can see."

Lucas saw through the bravado. He'd learned his lesson the day his house burned: the more frightened you are, the tougher you act. After the first fire, Lucas Gray Wolf had become the meanest five year old in existence. Three years later when the orphanage burned, he hadn't even shed a tear.

Finally his feet touched bottom, and Lucas was face-to-face with a red-haired, freckled-faced eight year old, none the worse for a few scratches and bruises, with a cowlick that defied all the laws of gravity and probably his mother's best efforts with a comb and brush. If he had a mother.

Lucas cut off the extra length of rope, stripped the cord out and began to fashion a rope ascender.

Rusty stuffed his hands in his pockets, tipped back on the heels of scruffy sneakers and announced, "You're bigger'n I thought you'd be."

"So are you. Now, let's get you out of here."

When Chuck Belinda had left her for a woman nearly half her age with a belly flat as a washboard and not a single child clinging to her thigh-high skirts, Mandy had thought good riddance, nobody is ever going to make me feel like a failure again.

And yet, here she was, standing in the sheriff's office at Pickwick, wringing her hands and telling how she had lost one of her children and feeling like the worst failure in the world. As well as the worst mother.

Her own mother had warned her. "Mandy Jean, if you go off into the woods with three children, I don't know what's going to become of you. There are snakes and bears and no telling what all up there."

The excuse she had given her mother seemed puny, now that Mandy could view it with hindsight. "Mother," she'd said, "I want my children to have every advantage they would if their father were living with them, and that includes camping. You worry too much."

Her mother had been right, of course. She so often was. And that was exactly why Mandy wasn't going to call her right away and say that she'd lost Rusty.

The sheriff peered at her through folds of fat with his

squinty black eyes. "Mrs. Belinda, are you sure this kid of yours is not just off playing on the riverbanks?"

"I looked. He's not there. He's not anywhere."

Mandy struggled to keep the rising panic out of her voice. Jill and Betsy were hanging on to her legs for dear life. No sense upsetting them even more.

"Now, let me get this straight, Mrs. Belinda. You said the last time you saw him was about ten this morning?"

"Yes. The girls were playing dolls in front of the tent, I was cleaning up the breakfast dishes, and Rusty told me he was going to pick some wild blackberries we'd seen growing up behind our campsite."

Sheriff Cranshaw looked at his watch. "That was only four hours ago. Officially, this boy of yours is not a missing person for twenty-four to forty-eight hours."

Mandy wanted to hit him with her purse. Her child was gone, and he was talking to her about points of law.

"Are you telling me you won't send a search party to look for my child?"

"Boys pull practical jokes like this all the time. He'll turn up by sundown. And if he doesn't, well, you just let us know and we'll send out a party first thing in the morning."

She thanked him as politely as she could, then marched out of there with her two little girls still hanging on for dear life. She had no intention of waiting till sundown.

"Pompous old goat," she muttered when she was in her car.

For once, Betsy didn't ask, "What's pompous?" Six, going on twenty-six, her daughter had the look of a Barbie doll and the mind of a Philadelphia lawyer. Three-year-old Jill merely scrunched into her seat and sucked harder on her thumb.

That was all Chuck's fault. Jill had been a sunny, well-adjusted little girl before he took off with that skinny floozy.

Mandy's mind whirled like a squirrel in a cage. The first thing she had to do was find her son. The sun was sinking fast and she didn't have a minute to lose.

"Now, girls, don't you worry about a thing. We're going back to find your brother."

She had no choice but to take them with her. There was no time to lose. Jill's smile was watery and Betsy's shaky.

"You're my brave little soldiers," Mandy said. Then she cranked the car and set out to find her son.

Rusty, sporting six new Band-Aids, sat by the campfire roasting marshmallows on a pronged stick and grinning like the Cheshire cat. He had eaten the two Snickers bars Lucas gave him when they first came out of the cave, as well as three he'd snitched from the backpack when Lucas wasn't looking. The evidence of his crime decorated his lips. He had steadfastly refused to give any information about himself.

"I run away and I ain't going back," he'd said, then clammed up.

Catching Lucas's eye, Rusty grinned. "Ain't this the life?" he said.

Lucas grunted. What else could he do? He couldn't leave the kid in the woods—though the idea was tempting.

When he'd tried to take Rusty into town to the sheriff's office, the kid had kicked and screamed and punched like a wildcat. Now Lucas had a bruise on his shin the size of a hen's egg and a miniature dictator sitting at his campfire.

So much for freedom. Tomorrow, he was taking the kid in if he had to hog-tie him.

Rusty glanced at the GoldWing bike, his eyes alight. "If I had me a machine like that, I'd head to Canada."

Lucas made a mental note to lock it up tight and sleep with the key. It wouldn't surprise him if the kid tried to steal the bike.

"You can get that idea out of your head. We're leaving first thing in the morning, but not to Canada."

"Not to no sheriff's office, either."

Lucas refused to get into an argument with an eight year old. The indomitable Rusty reinforced Lucas's decision to remain unattached. He'd been with Rusty only a couple of hours and already he could tell that he would have made a lousy parent.

"You can have the bedroll tonight, Rusty."

"Where will you sleep?"

"I'll just curl up in a blanket." He'd been doing it all his life. The first fire caused him to decide that living in structures that could burn to the ground was a dangerous thing, and the second fire had reinforced that opinion.

Lucas spread the bedroll in the shelter of the trees. "The sky's clear. You won't have to worry about getting wet."

"I ain't worried about getting wet, and I ain't going to bed. I ain't sleepy."

"Ain't is bad grammar."

"You ain't my daddy."

"Who is your father?"

"I ain't got one."

It was the first bit of useful information Lucas had gleaned from the kid, though there was always the possibility that Rusty wasn't telling the truth.

Since asking direct questions didn't work, Lucas decided to be cagey. He picked up a stick and started whittling.

"What're you making?"

"A whistle." Silence. Out of the corner of his eye, Lucas could see Rusty thinking this over.

"You got a horse?"

"I'll answer your question if you'll answer one for me."

Rusty stuffed his hands into his pockets and stomped off into the woods. Lucas called his bluff. In spite of the full moon, the woods at night didn't look like a friendly place for a child. Not fifty feet away, Rusty turned around and came back. Plopping down, he scowled at Lucas.

"This don't mean I'm gonna stay here."

"Good. I travel alone."

An owl called from the darkness, and Rusty eased closer to Lucas. That small gesture made Lucas's heart do funny things. When the chips were down, Rusty was nothing more than a little boy alone in the woods with a stranger.

"I have lots of horses," Lucas said. "I own a ranch out West."

"Wow."

Lucas put a gentle hand on the little boy's arm. "What's your mother's name, Rusty?"

"I ain't telling." His chin quivered and there was a hint of moisture in his eyes, but Rusty stared staunchly ahead, as if he were seeing visions no one else could see, and hearing a distant tune with an offbeat that he loved.

"Bedtime, kid."

This time, Rusty didn't argue. Lucas watched the bag swallow up the little boy till nothing was visible but the tip of his nose and the top of his head.

Was his mother abusive? Is that why he had run away?

If he thought this kid had been abused by anybody, he'd be damned if he'd take him back.

One reason Lucas loved wide-open spaces was that so-called civilization spawned evil deeds such as abuse and kidnapping and murder. Nature acted as a buffer. Lucas lay down on his blanket and stared up at the stars until everything fell into perspective.

Tomorrow he would find out about the child, one way or another.

Mandy Belinda wasn't the kind of woman to take defeat easily, but the task of finding an eight-year-old boy in thousands of acres of woods was daunting. She'd never been a Girl Scout, never been an outdoorswoman. She hadn't even owned a compass before this camping trip, and maps boggled her mind.

When she and Chuck had traveled—not that they had ever gone anywhere, except up to Memphis to take the kids to the zoo and over to Huntsville so Chuck could tour the Space and Rocket Center—he had always read the maps.

She circled the camp, fanning out, but the going was slow with the girls. She yelled Rusty's name until she was hoarse, but the only response was a deep echoing silence.

When Jill stumbled over a root and began to cry, Mandy felt like crying herself. Instead she went back to camp, fed her girls and tucked them in, then went to bed with her clothes on. Closing her eyes, she prayed that somewhere, somehow, her son was safe.

The rock hit Lucas in the back and brought him out of sleep with a jerk. Rusty stood nearby with a fistful of rocks, the sky behind him faint pink with dawn.

"What are you doing, kid? Trying to kill me so you can steal my bike?"

"Naw. I'm trying to kill that big old rattlesnake coiled up on your blanket." Lucas vaulted out of his blanket and Rusty doubled over with laughter. "April Fool!"

Lucas grinned. He'd pulled worse pranks than that at the orphanage. Years ago he'd gone back to apologize to Miss Jane Whitcomb, the housemother, for all the frogs and spiders he'd put in her sheets and under her teacups.

"It's June," Lucas said.

"Yeah, but I fooled you, didn't I?".

"You did. Are you hungry?"

"Naw. I already ate."

A circle of chocolate ringed the boy's mouth. Lucas knew without looking that he'd stolen the rest of the Snicker's bars. What amazed Lucas was that he'd slept through the whole thing. Two years ago, a twig snapping would have brought him out of sleep. A whisper. Even a footfall on grass. Suddenly, forty felt old.

"Find yourself another target, Rusty, and don't go out of sight. I'm having breakfast, then we'll take a ride."

"Whoopee!" Suspicion quickly replaced celebration. "Not to no sheriff's office."

"Do you want to ride or not?" The boy's face mirrored his struggle. "I guess not." Lucas sat on a log and began to eat his breakfast bar.

Rusty sidled up to him and sat on the opposite end of the log, whistling. Little by little he inched closer.

"If me and you can ride a little while, I'll show you my mama's camp."

Lucas wasn't ready to strike deals yet. "Why did you run away?" If he'd been abused, Lucas was headed straight for the law.

Rusty stuck out his chin and started whistling "Who's

Afraid of the Big Bad Wolf,'' which Lucas recognized immediately. One of Lucas's quirks was that he knew the name of practically every song that had ever been written, and the words to most of them.

''Was somebody mean to you, kid?'' he asked softly.

Rusty jumped up and balled his hands into fists. ''My mama ain't mean, and I'll fight anybody who says she is.''

''Whoa, now.'' Lucas took his arm. ''I didn't say she was mean. I'm just asking why you ran away.''

'''Cause I ain't got nobody but girls in my family, and all they do is play dolls and cook. I like adventure.''

Standing up, Lucas suppressed his grin. ''All right, Rusty, let's break camp. We'll ride twenty minutes, and no arguing. Your mother must be worried sick about you.''

Fifteen minutes later, they were on the GoldWing headed south along the river. The extra helmet Lucas carried in case he found somebody interesting in his travels, namely a woman, was too big for Rusty, but it was better than nothing.

Lucas came upon the woman suddenly, just as he topped the ridge near the cave where he'd found Rusty. She looked as if she'd come from combat in a small and dusty country. Her red hair was disheveled, her cheeks were smudged, and her shirttail was untucked. She had a miniature replica of herself perched on one hip and had another angelic child by the hand.

When she saw them, she stashed her daughters, then took up a wide-legged stance in front of her little girls, a she-bear getting ready to fight for her young.

It looked as if Lucas had found Rusty's mother. He brought his bike to a halt.

"If you come near me or my girls I'll make you sorry you were ever born," she said.

Lucas smiled. "Rusty's already done that. This morning."

"Don't try to con me. You let my son go."

She raised the stick, and Lucas suppressed a laugh. She was so tiny he could easily tuck her under his arm and carry her off if he wanted to. Which he absolutely did not. No matter how appealing that gleaming cap of red-gold curls was. What in the world would he do with a woman with three children?

Protect her.

The minute the thought whispered through his mind, Lucas knew he was in trouble. If anybody needed protection, it was Rusty's mom. The little redhead, who'd appeared from behind a bush, was sitting on the ground behind her sucking her thumb, clinging to her baby doll and crying, and the little blond standing beside her sister looked as if she didn't know whether to fight or cry.

And Lucas already knew enough about the hellion on his motorbike to feel enormous sympathy for the woman facing him with a stick half as big as she was.

"My name is Lucas Gray Wolf. I rescued your son from the bottom of a cave."

She wavered between disbelief and gratitude. "That's a likely story. Rusty, come here."

Ignoring her, Rusty sat on the bike as if it were a throne from which he planned to rule for the next six years. The tiny dynamo with the stick took a step closer to Lucas.

"You let my son go."

Swiveling, Lucas plucked Rusty off the motorcycle, then dismounted. "Be a good boy and go to your mother."

Rusty didn't budge. Instead, he caught hold of the handlebars and held on for dear life. "Me and Gray Wolf's going to Canada."

"You're doing no such thing."

The woman rushed Lucas so fast, he barely had time to sidestep. He caught the end of the stick as it whistled past his chest. The spitfire at the other end held on for dear life, glaring at him.

"Rusty, tell your mother I didn't kidnap you."

"He put a sack over my head while I was picking berries, Mama. I kicked and screamed, but he was too big for me."

The woman dropped the end of the stick and lunged for Lucas's face. He caught her wrists, and they felt like bird bones, so fragile he was afraid he would break them.

Up close, he could see a fine line of golden freckles dusting her cheeks. Her nose was uptilted, and her eyes were as green as the willows that bend over the Verde River in the late evening breezes.

Cleaned up, she was probably beautiful. If he cared. Which he definitely did not.

Lucas nearly lost his grip when she hauled off and kicked his shin. She was stronger than she looked.

"Be still," he said. "I'm afraid I'll break your wrists."

"I'll just bet you are. Barbarian!" With that she bit his hand.

There was nothing to do except haul her in so tight she couldn't move. As he held her prisoner in his arms, he was surprised at how good she felt.

She was shocked speechless. Almost.

"I didn't kidnap your child, lady. As a matter of fact, I'll pay you to take him back."

Rusty was thoroughly enjoying the show, and even his little sisters were looking as if they might smile.

"How much you gonna give for me, Gray Wolf?"

The woman in his arms suddenly stopped struggling. Apparently, it had dawned on her that Rusty was having too much fun for a kid who had been kidnapped.

"Rusty Belinda, you tell me the truth this minute, or when I get you back home you'll be the sorriest little boy on the block."

"Aw, Mama."

"I'm not kidding. I want the truth and I want it now." Rusty was silent. "Did this man kidnap you?"

"Naw. I run off 'cause I was sick of *girls*. Then I was gonna explore this ole cave, see? Gray Wolf got me out, but I could'a got out by myself."

"I will deal with you later, young man."

When she tipped her head to look up at him, Lucas had to fight the urge to wipe the smudge from her cheek.

"I owe you an apology," she said.

"No harm done."

"Yes, there is. I smacked you with a stick and bit your hand."

He grinned. "The acorn doesn't fall far from the tree."

"Oh, my Lord. I don't even want to know what he did."

Her smile transformed her. It was brilliant, flashing across her face like a comet leaving a trail of light that turned the centers of her eyes golden. Lucas felt off balance and more than a little uncomfortable.

He was too old to start revising his opinions about life in general and women in particular. For years he'd believed life was to be led solo, and that women were like bus stops: if you missed the first one, the second was just over the horizon.

He'd tried really hard to change with Gloria, the doctor who'd patched him up after a stallion he was taming got the best of him. Two years later both of them knew it would never work. Hurt pride didn't matter. It was the hurting heart that nearly did him in.

"You can let go now," she said.

"What?"

"I said, you can let go now. I won't bite."

She already had. Lucas might bear the scar a long time.

He released her and stepped apart quickly, as if he had never thought about the warmth and appeal of a small, cuddly woman.

"I'm afraid I've been very rude to you, Mr. Gray Wolf."

"Call me Lucas. Please."

"And I'm Mandy, Mandy Belinda."

She offered a hand as delicate as a rose. His hand swallowed hers, and suddenly he felt as if he might be ten feet tall. He quickly turned his attention to her little girls just to get away from the dazzle of Mandy Belinda's smile.

"These must be your daughters," he said.

"Yes. Betsy, the oldest, and Jill." She held out her arms. "Come here, darlings, and say hello to this nice man who found your brother."

The little girls raced over, their faces wreathed in the bewitching smiles they'd learned from their mother. Lucas was dazzled all over again.

"Thank you," they chorused, and when they caught his hands he wondered why he had ever thought he wasn't cut out for fatherhood. What could be so hard about taking care of two angels? Three, he added to himself, glancing at their mother.

Mandy Belinda smiled at him again, and that's when he knew he was in real trouble.

"How can we ever thank you, Lucas?"

His name dripped off her tongue like warm honey, and he wanted to hear her say it again, but he dared not ask. He dared not do anything except stand still and try to learn how to breathe again.

"It was my pleasure," he said, and he guessed if he'd been wearing a hat he would have tipped it. If he'd been wearing a coat, he'd have spread it on the ground for her to walk on, whether or not there was a puddle. If they had been in a ballroom with French doors leading to the balcony, he'd have knocked every other man out of the way just for the privilege of opening the door for her. Mandy Belinda was that kind of woman.

"I have some homemade brownies back at the camp. Do say you'll come and share a brownie with us. It's the least I can do."

If she'd offered him a meal, he might have declined. If she'd offered him a cool drink, hot as it was, he might have had the sense to say no. But she was offering him the one thing he couldn't resist—chocolate.

"I'd like that," he said, knowing all the time that he should get on his bike and ride the other way as fast as he could, knowing that if she smiled at him in that sparkly way again he was going to be in big trouble.

That's how he ended up at her campsite, sitting at a picnic table provided by the park, eating the best brownies he'd ever put in his mouth and watching Mandy with more than passing interest.

Suddenly it was very important to find out whether Rusty had been telling the truth about not having a father!

Mandy, you're out of your mind. That's what she kept telling herself.

For one thing, she didn't know a bit of the history attached to Lucas Gray Wolf, and any Southerner worth their salt insisted on knowing the entire family tree before they sat down to eat with a stranger. For another, he was wild looking in an exotic, heart-stopping kind of way, and he was traveling around on an evil-looking machine which didn't get one whit tamer for having been parked beside her Honda Civic.

Of course, he *had* rescued Rusty, and then he'd gallantly escorted them back through the woods, carrying Jill, for which Mandy would be forever grateful. Rusty had pitched a fit about not getting to ride the motorcycle, but somehow one look from Lucas Gray Wolf quelled that temper tantrum. Later, he'd explained that he had only one extra helmet, and he never let people ride without a helmet.

Which was fine by Mandy. Just being around the man was enough to make her heart jump into her throat. She couldn't imagine what it would be like to sit behind him on that powerful machine and go roaring through the woods. Like something wild. Like something that would keep her awake at night in a tizzy of excitement.

And so he'd brought them all back to camp, then gone back alone for his motorcycle.

"These are the best brownies I ever ate," he said, reaching for a second. And then, "May I?"

"Of course." She was as pleased as if she'd won the Betty Crocker award.

"Did you say you make these?"

"Yes. I bake and sell goodies in a little shop I call Lucky Mandy's."

"Nice name," he said. "Unusual."

"I guess I'm the last of the eternal optimists. I decided a name like that was bound to be good for business."

"I'm sure it has been...for you and your husband."

Mandy flushed. It sounded as if Lucas Gray Wolf were

fishing to find out whether she had a husband. That was absolutely ridiculous, of course. Why would a man like Lucas be interested in a woman like her? With those amazing blue eyes, that untamed dark hair and those shoulders that went on forever, he was what all the slick women's magazines called a hunk. Hunks went for women with twenty-two inch waistlines and washboard bellies and bleached blond hair. They went for women who giggled a lot and batted their eyelashes and flattered them with pretty lies.

They definitely did not go for women with an independent streak as big as Oklahoma, a tart tongue, a stretch-marked belly and hair that looked as if it had been styled with an egg beater. And they most certainly didn't go for a woman with three challenging, demanding, rambunctious children. Even if they were angels. Usually.

Still, she liked the rush of excitement that came from thinking Lucas *might* be interested in her. After all, he loved her brownies, so who was to say he might not want something different in a woman, somebody with a brain and talents that extended beyond the bedroom?

She could dream, couldn't she? And so, just as bold as could be, she said to him, "I don't have a husband."

"I'm sorry," he said, but he didn't look sorry at all. In fact, he looked rather pleased, and that fueled Mandy's fire even more.

What if this rakish man, who obviously loved to live dangerously, had actually been traveling across the country for years searching for a woman exactly like Mandy? A woman who would smooth back his hair and press tender kisses on his forehead, a woman who would cuddle up to him under Grandmother Bailey's quilts and whisper endearments to him, a woman who would scrub his back in the shower without any expectations at all, a woman who would do those things simply for the joy of it? What if he wanted a woman like that?

And what if the moon were made of green cheese?

Mandy sighed. Her mother called her an impossible dreamer, and she guessed she was. Still, what did it hurt to reach for the stars? If she got lucky, she might catch one someday.

"Another brownie?"

"Just one more, then I have to go."

Lucas's hand brushed hers when she passed him the plate, and she felt such a tingle she suddenly wished she were alone in the woods with him. Given his extraordinary looks and her enforced state of deprivation, that didn't surprise Mandy a bit.

Sometimes she wished she were the kind of woman who leaped before she looked. Sometimes she wished she were the kind of woman who didn't always have to look a gift horse in the mouth.

She wasn't, of course. She was sensible and mature and reliable. She was steadfast and hardworking and rarely spontaneous. In fact, she couldn't remember a spontaneous thing she'd done in the last two years. Not since Chuck left.

In the distance, her two oldest children were racing around the meadow playing tag, their laughter lifting like kites. Inside the tent, Jill was curled into a ball with her doll, taking a nap.

Beside her was Lucas Gray Wolf. The most appealing man she was likely to meet. Ever. And he was going to get on his motorcycle and ride right out of her life.

"You can't go," she said, and her boldness surprised her as much as it did him.

"I've imposed on your hospitality too long," he responded. "I'm sure you have better things to do than sit at a picnic table chatting with me."

It was the most exciting thing she'd done since she rode the roller coaster in Memphis with Chuck on their first date, but she didn't tell Lucas that. Instead she invented a smooth excuse to keep him, right on the spot, which amazed her. She wasn't that kind of woman, either, the kind given to invention for ulterior purposes.

"You can't go until I look at your wounds. I should have already put ice on your shin, and I read somewhere that the human bite is more dangerous than a dog bite."

His laughter was rich and deep and thrilling. Wouldn't it be lovely to sit on the porch swing with him in the evenings after the children were tucked into bed and say something so brilliant and witty that he would fill the darkness with his laughter!

Her toes curled under at the thought, and she smiled at him because he was that kind of man, the kind that made a woman want to smile.

"I'm sure I'll live…"

Dear goodness, he was going to turn her down, and then she'd be left in these woods by herself with three children she never should have brought here in the first place.

"…however, I wouldn't mind if you take a look at my so-called wounds."

"The first-aid kit is in the tent."

"I don't want to disturb your daughter."

"Jill could sleep through a herd of elephants tromping through the tent."

Catching his hand to lead him was the most natural gesture in the world for her, considering how often she did it with her children. Immediately she saw the error of her ways. As well as the beauty.

He glanced down at her hand, then gently closed his around it. Was the sun suddenly brighter? The sky bluer? The air sweeter?

Lucas held the tent flap back, then ducked inside, a big man who filled the tent. And Mandy had to learn to breathe all over again.

She tilted her head back, their eyes met, and she was Alice stepping through the looking glass. There were wonders to behold, magical potions to sample, and unspoken promises that made her head spin.

"Why don't you sit down?" she murmured. "You're so big."

"And you're so small."

His fingers lightly traced her cheek, or was she dreaming with her eyes wide open? She held his gaze until she felt dizzy, then she fumbled in her backpack for the first-aid kit. She was glad her back was to him, glad he couldn't see how her hands were shaking.

Lord, what had possessed her to invite this mouth-watering hunk into her tent? What if she had misjudged him, and he was going to rip her clothes off and do wicked things to her?

Mandy bit back a groan. She longed for every wicked thing he might do.

Chapter Two

Lucas had expected to be on the Tennessee River with his fishing pole instead of sitting in Mandy Belinda's tent letting her tend his bogus wounds. But the fact was, he couldn't imagine being anywhere else, including on Paradise Ranch in Arizona.

Thundering through the canyons on his stallion paled beside Mandy holding his hand. Standing atop a butte with a million stars shining on his uplifted face didn't compare to feeling the soft brush of Mandy's hair as she inspected the bite.

She stuck the tip of her tongue between her lips in concentration. "I barely broke the skin," she said. "That's good."

"That's very good," he murmured, never taking his eyes off the line of moisture she'd left on her bottom lip.

"I'll swab it, though, just in case."

"Hmm." He was still concentrating on her lips. When

she talked they made a perfect heart shape. Lucas was intrigued. What would they taste like?

"This might sting a little."

She could have burned his hand off and he wouldn't have noticed. He was concentrating on a tiny bead of sweat that rolled down her forehead and hung on her eyelash like a raindrop. She blinked and the bit of moisture dropped onto his hand. He fought an urge to catch it with his tongue.

"It feels nice," he said, but he wasn't talking about the antiseptic.

"I'm used to this kind of thing. Jill or Betsy or Rusty is always coming to me with a wound in need of attention. Thank goodness it usually requires nothing more than a Band-Aid and a kiss to make it better."

"Do I get a kiss to make it better?" His smile was innocent but his heart was full of guile.

"Of course."

The color flagging her cheeks belied her flippant reply. And when she brushed her lips against his hand, he felt as if he'd been touched by angel wings. The shock sent his mind reeling. Until that moment, he had never felt magic in a kiss.

Do it again, he wanted to say. Instead, he said, "Your children are very lucky."

That brought another wash of color to her lovely cheeks. Then, because she was so near and so irresistible, he cupped her chin and tenderly rubbed away the smudge on her left cheekbone.

"Oh my," she whispered.

"I've been wanting to do that since I first saw you."

Watching her reaction, he held his breath. Would she take his statement as a ploy to get into her good graces, or would she see it for what it was, an unexpected truth that was both premature and somewhat embarrassing?

An apology was on the tip of his tongue when she said, "Thank you."

Her words were soft and sweet and Lucas knew he had met the most dangerous woman he would ever encounter: a genuine human being. There was no artifice in Mandy. Underneath that rumpled white blouse beat a pure heart.

"You're more than welcome," he said, then he withdrew his hands, not because he wanted to, but because of her dignity and her endearing sincerity.

Mandy made him remember dreams long forgotten. She made him long for all the things he'd missed: love with a soft, sweet woman, children, family.

The air between them shimmered with longing, and her pulse beat wildly in her slender throat. He yearned to put his lips there, right at the base of her neck, and he knew in his bones how she would taste—like cream and honey.

Suddenly, something wary and skittish reared its ugly head in Lucas, and he knew he was very close to doing something he would regret. Mandy saved him.

"Now, let me look at that shin of yours, but don't expect me to get on my knees and kiss it."

Laughter was a relief to both of them.

"Not even a friendly peck?" he said, teasing her.

"Not even that. I don't pucker up for just any old thing, you know."

He rolled up the legs of his blue jeans, and she bent over him, more to hide her flushed face, he suspected, than to inspect his shin.

"You're going to have a bruise."

Thankfully, she refrained from putting her hands on

his legs. There was only so much exquisite torture he
could stand.

"I'll get some ice." She hurried from the tent.

Like a deep-sea diver who had been deprived of oxy-
gen, Lucas drew a long breath. What was he doing in
Mandy Belinda's tent like a smitten schoolboy with his
britches' leg turned up? Rolling stones gather no moss
had always been his motto. As soon as she came back
he would politely accept the ice pack, then get on his
GoldWing and head for the hills.

The minute he saw her face, Lucas's plans flew out
the window. Tears of distress stood in her eyes, and her
lower lip trembled like a child's.

"There's no ice," she said.

"I really don't need any."

"Somebody left the top off the ice chest and now everything's ruined. All the food, the juice…oh, what will
we eat?"

She gulped back a sob, and Lucas pictured himself
mounting his black stallion and riding to her rescue. What
he did, actually, was slide his arm around her slender
shoulders. To offer comfort, he told himself. But the minute his skin made contact with hers, he became so much
more than comforter. He became savage, a beast who
would tear the heart out of anything who dared threaten
her. More than that, Lucas become a hero.

"Don't you worry about a thing, Mandy. I'll race to
the nearest convenience store for supplies, and then I'll
catch us a nice big mess of fish for dinner." He patted
her arm, rubbed her shoulders and squeezed her hand in
reassurance. "How does that sound?"

"Would you?"

"Yes, I've been longing to give my pole a good work-
out."

She turned scarlet to the roots of her hair, and he backed off like a stuttering schoolboy.

"That would be so lovely," she said. He got hot thinking how *lovely* it would be. "Are you sure you don't mind? We've already been so much trouble."

"I would walk through hell for one more taste…" Was that stars in her eyes, or was he merely projecting? For a while, he got lost in the glow. Then he added much, much too late. "A taste of your brownies."

"All right then, it's a deal. Off to the store you go."

"Do you want to make a list?"

"A list?"

"Of things you need."

"Oh, of course." Bent over her paper with her tongue caught between her teeth, she was an enticing sight. Lucas had to remind himself why he was staying.

He would bring in supplies, catch their dinner, perhaps share it with them and then be on his way. Free as a bird. No attachments. No regrets.

"Can I go fishing with you, Lucas?" Rusty said.

"Me, too," Betsy chimed in.

"Me, too," Jill said.

Lucas's first reaction was to say no. Fishing was a solitary pursuit, something a man did when he wanted to be alone with his thoughts and the river. But three eager little faces were turned in Lucas's direction, and he remembered how it had been when he was a boy. He used to long for a father to fish with, but he would never have admitted it aloud. Not to a soul.

How could he deny these fatherless children? Besides, Mandy was looking at him with such glowing expectation that he'd have walked over hot coals before disappointing her.

"Sure," he said. "Grab your poles."

"I don't have a pole," Jill said, and began to cry.

What could he do but pick her up and hug her? Lucas had always been helpless before a female's tears.

"That's all right, sweetheart. You can share mine."

"Can I?" Jill pressed a cheek as soft as duck's down against his. Lucas's heart grew to twice its normal size.

"Absolutely. Why, I'll bet you'll catch the biggest fish of all."

"You're very good with children," Mandy said. He didn't want to be good with children. Lucas didn't want to be anything except what he was—a man who traveled light and traveled alone.

But Mandy was watching him with a face that shone as if she'd scrubbed it with moonbeams. He could do nothing but smile.

"Come on, Lucas," Rusty yelled. "Down yonder there's a catfish big as my leg." He raced ahead to the river with Betsy in his wake yelling, "Wait for me."

"It looks as if we're being left behind." Lucas offered his arm to Mandy. "Shall we join them?"

The air was soft, the child cuddly, and the woman sweet smelling. A long stretch of lonely years trailed behind him, and for a moment, Lucas ached for what might have been.

They came upon the water suddenly. There was a natural bend in the river where ancient oaks cast a shade over the water and years of overflow had created a sandy beach perfect for frolicking, as well as fishing.

Rusty and Betsy staked out a spot for themselves. Lucas cast the fishing line for Jill while Mandy kicked off her shoes, rolled up her jeans and laughed when the sand squished between her toes. Lucas couldn't keep his eyes off her. Jill, sitting in his lap fishing, didn't notice.

"I got one," she squealed. Lucas helped her reel in what turned out to be a little more than a fingerling. "Look, Mommy, I got one."

"So you did, sweetheart." When Mandy squatted beside them, soft and fragrant, Lucas wanted to bury his face in the curve of her neck and inhale. "But I think this one's too small. Maybe we should throw him back."

"No! He's mine."

"Don't you want him to grow up big?"

"No. I want to eat him."

Lucas laughed. "A child after my own heart."

"Don't encourage her." Jill turned a wide-eyed look on him that was so clearly manipulative, Lucas had to suppress another laugh. "See. I told you," Mandy added, but she was having a hard time not laughing, too.

"Can I keep him, Lucas?"

"I tell you what, sweetheart, let's throw this little bitty thing back so he can be with his mama, and I'll help you catch a big one. How's about that?"

"Okay." Jill favored her mother with a look of pure triumph.

"This I've got to see."

Mandy settled comfortably beside him, her toes buried in the sand, her thigh bumping against his. The river whispered by, the sun warmed his back and the breeze stirred the air. Nearby, Rusty and Betsy conversed in clear, flute-like voices. With the child in his arms and Mandy's sweet weight against his leg, Lucas was as content as he'd ever been.

So this is what it's like to have a family.

A man could get used to it.

The moon was round and as yellow as a hoop of cheese, the night air was sweet with honeysuckle, her children were in bed fast asleep, and Lucas Gray Wolf was sitting at her campfire gazing at her as if she were the most beautiful woman on earth and wonderful, besides. For the first time since childhood, Mandy believed in fairy godmothers.

How else could she explain a perfect evening, the end to an almost perfect day? How else could she explain why a man as devilishly attractive as Lucas was still with her instead of a hundred miles away on his mean machine?

"That was the best fish dinner I've ever had," he said.

"Thanks to you. I don't know how you managed to catch so many in such a short time. You're an expert fisherman."

He had the look of a man who was expert at everything he did. Even kissing. *Especially* kissing. Wouldn't it be wonderful if she could find out?

She was being silly, of course. Just because he spent all afternoon with her three children at the river patiently teaching them how to fish, didn't mean he was interested in fanning Mandy's flames.

She giggled at herself. The way she was sizzling merely sitting beside him, it wouldn't take much to turn her into a blazing inferno.

"What's so funny?" Lucas asked.

"Me. I'm such a silly dreamer."

"On the contrary, you're a beautiful dreamer." He sang the opening bars of Stephen Foster's "Beautiful Dreamer" in a very good baritone. Suddenly he stopped, abashed. "I do that. I know the lyrics to practically every song I've ever heard. It's a curse."

"I'd call it a gift."

"You're sweet."

His compliment was balm to her battered soul. It

rained like warm honey over the stress of raising three children alone. It cascaded like cool waters over the anxiety of her only son lost in the woods. It poured like sweet wine over every ugly thing Chuck had ever said and done to her, including walking out on her without so much as a farewell. The coward had called her from a truck stop in Texas, on his way to Reno for a quickie divorce. The love of his life was at his side, he'd said, which had only added insult to injury.

Mandy was so full it would have taken an act of Congress to stop her tears.

"Hey, now, I didn't mean to make you cry."

Men were sometimes totally clueless. Even men as fabulous as Lucas Gray Wolf.

"It's not you. It's everything." She scrubbed at her face with the back of her hand, but the tears kept coming. Any minute now, she figured she'd see Lucas leaving through a blur of mascara. "Twice in one day. You must think I'm a horrible crybaby."

His hug caught her by surprise. And it wasn't one of those wimpy hugs, either, the kind where it was clear that the hugger was merely being polite to the huggee. Lucas held her solidly against his chest, his arms strong and tight, his hand cradling the back of her head, his chin resting on her hair. It was the kind of hug she'd coveted for years. It was the kind of hug dreams were made of.

"It's been a hell of a time for you," he said. "I would be more surprised if you didn't cry."

"You would?" She tried to twist around to see his face, but he held her tight, which was fine with her. Better than fine. Being embraced by Lucas was absolutely the most wonderful sensation she'd had since she'd discovered sex.

"I would." He wove his fingers through her hair, and

it felt just right. "Let me tell you a story. One night when I was five years old, I woke up and started searching for my dog. Old Jimmy always slept by my bed, and when I couldn't find him, I assumed he had gone off into the woods chasing rabbits or his ancient dreams of rabbits."

She loved the way he told a story, his voice rising and falling in a lovely cadence that was music to her starving soul.

"I found my dog trying to corner a skunk, but while I was in the woods my house burned. My parents and my baby brother never woke up."

"That must have been horrible for you. I'm so sorry."

The thought of the child Lucas losing his entire family brought fresh tears that wet the front of his shirt. He pulled her so close that she was practically in his lap.

"Then, when I was eight, the orphanage I was in burned, and I would have, too, if I hadn't been outside with my dog sneaking a smoke."

"Oh my. What a tragedy. Was anyone killed?"

"Three children were trapped inside. One of them was my friend, Janice."

Mandy squeezed him so hard and close she could feel the pounding of his heart. It was a steady, comforting rhythm.

"I didn't cry until I was grown. Instead, I became a hellion. I was so bad that no foster family would keep me for more than six months."

Mandy sneaked a peek at his motorcycle. Only the very successful could afford such an expensive bike, but if the truth were told, Lucas Gray Wolf was probably still a hellion, or at least a rebel.

"Like my own son. He's never cried about his daddy leaving, though I know it must be preying on his mind."

"Poor little kid." Lucas tenderly wiped her tears with

the tips of his fingers. "So you see, Mandy, I don't think you're a silly crybaby at all. I think you're an emotionally healthy woman venting your feelings."

Not all of them, she thought. Basking in the warmth of Lucas's affirmation and his embrace, she transformed from a tearful woman to a hopeful one. Wouldn't it be lovely if she could persuade Lucas to stay? Just for one night. One glorious night so she could see the shape of a caring man in his bedroll and hear the comforting sounds of his breathing. She didn't mind if he snored. In fact, she would welcome it. All those manly snorts and deep growls that sent a message, plain and clear: there's a man in the house.

Or, in this case, in the woods.

Was that asking too much?

Lucas decided there was magic in the moon. Or perhaps it was a devil, just like the song said. Otherwise why was he still sitting beside Mandy's campfire when the open road was so close and the night breeze so cool?

Lucas loved night riding. After dark, the world took on a tranquility it didn't have during the waking hours. In daylight, people rushed about, frantic and stressed, so caught up in their hurly-burly routines they didn't have time to slow down for something as simple as watching a sunrise.

Or smelling a rose. Or hugging a soft, desirable woman.

Mandy was all that and more. She was intensely alive and totally unafraid to express genuine feelings.

He pictured how she'd looked standing on the riverbank with her jeans rolled up and her bare feet sinking into the mud, laughing as Lucas dodged flying fishhooks from Betsy's first attempts at casting. He'd seen the tenderness on her face as she'd tried to convince Jill to throw back the minnow-sized fish Lucas had helped her catch. And her pride when Rusty had offered her his arm on their walk back to camp.

How could he bear to leave a woman like that? Especially when she'd so recently been weeping.

He was casting about in his mind, trying to think of a good excuse to stay, when Mandy rescued him.

"It's getting late. I wish you would stay the night."

The invitation was probably nothing except a manifestation of the good manners of a polite woman, but Lucas read more into it. He read genuine kindness and a touch of loneliness and perhaps a bit of old-fashioned yearning.

"You're right. It is late. No need to leave now. The road will still be there in the morning."

She tilted her face toward his, and when he saw how her eyes shone, he bent down to kiss her. How could he resist?

He tested the heart shape of her lips, and they were sweet, as he'd known they would be, as sweet as thick cream with freshly gathered clover honey from a million bees. She kissed with soft open lips, and when her tongue touched his it was so hot it burned.

The heady combination of innocence and eroticism spawned such a storm of passion in Lucas that he almost lost control. And wouldn't that be a terrible thing to do to Mandy Belinda: add the indignity of fighting off a man with his hormones in overdrive to the stress of almost losing her son?

Blame the moon, he thought, then tear himself away, even if it killed him.

She must have sensed his turmoil, for Mandy pulled back, saving him all kinds of embarrassment.

"I would offer you a place to sleep in the tent, but with three children, it's kind of crowded in there."

"That's all right. I always sleep in a bedroll under the stars."

"Always?"

"Except in the most inclement weather. It's safer that way."

He was glad she didn't ask safer from what? A question like that might have led to all sorts of discussion about stolen kisses and pent-up passion and temptation so great it was bound to steal a man's sleep.

"Well, then," she said, smiling at him.

She was so beautiful, he wanted to kiss her again. And not stop till he had his fill.

Was it possible to get his fill of a woman like Mandy Belinda? Lucas didn't plan to stick around and find out. He was leaving first thing in the morning. Before daylight.

"I hope you'll stay for breakfast in the morning."

"Of course," he said, reckless fool that he was. "Thank you."

"You're welcome." It was her smile that was his undoing. Or was it the heat that flashed through him when she touched his cheek? "Good night, Lucas Gray Wolf."

"Good night, Mandy Belinda."

What was an evening farewell without a kiss to dream on?

When his lips touched hers once more, her arms stole around his neck and she moved into him as naturally as if she were born to be there. Her body molded perfectly into the contours of his, even if he did have to lift her off her feet a bit to make it happen.

The kiss was long and deep, and Mandy softly murmured her satisfaction. If her three children hadn't been sleeping in the tent nearby, he'd have covered her with his blanket and made love to her until the moon vanished in the first pink blush of dawn.

Lucas was on fire, and this time he couldn't blame it on the moon.

Chapter Three

Mandy knew women who could kiss a man, then go about their business as if nothing had happened. There were even women who made jokes about the number of men they'd kissed, women who rated the opposite sex on a scale of one to ten, according to the man's expertise in kissing.

Well, thank goodness, she was not one of those women. She lay in her bedroll with her face to the tent flap so she could see Lucas through the opening. The memory of his kisses still burned through her; and she knew that if she lived to be a hundred and two like her great-aunt Mandybell for whom she was named, she would never forget her first kiss with Lucas Gray Wolf.

Nor the second, either. It was the second one that was almost her undoing. For a crazy moment, she'd almost forgotten who she was and where she was.

Jill stirred beside her, fretful in her sleep after a day

filled with so much excitement. Mandy rubbed her child's back.

Tomorrow she would head home. They'd had enough excitement for one camping trip.

Outside her tent, Lucas Gray Wolf lay in his blanket, silvery and mysterious, carved by the moon. The thought of saying goodbye to him wrenched Mandy's heart.

He'd said he was on the road going wherever whim took him. Maybe she would invite him to come home with her for a home-cooked dinner. It was the least she could do to thank him, wasn't it?

Lucas had only meant to stay through breakfast. Then Jill had climbed into his lap to show him her doll, and Betsy had made him a crown of clover, and before he knew it, Rusty was gathering sticks and consulting him on which one would make the best whistles, and the sun was riding high in the sky.

"What do you think about this one, Lucas?" Rusty asked.

"That one is too thin. You need one thick enough to carve out the inside."

"Reckon you could show me how?"

"I reckon I could."

"That's gonna take a while, wouldn't you figure?"

"Probably so. But I'll bet you're a fast learner, Rusty."

"Naw. Sometimes I'm slow as molasses. I bet it'll take you three or four weeks to teach me how to make a whistle. But you promised."

"Rusty." Mandy was sweet and lovely, even when she chided her son. With a jolt Lucas realized he hated to tell her goodbye.

"I was thinking," she said to Lucas, "since you're

leaving today and we're also leaving, why don't you come home with us and stay a little while? At least for dinner.''

"Yeah!'' Rusty shouted. "And me and you can ride that big ole motorcycle of yours.''

"Please, Lucas.'' Jill wrapped her arms around his neck and pressed a cheek as soft as a duck's down against his. "Please.''

Were the gods smiling on him or playing a dirty trick? He couldn't turn down Mandy's invitation without seeming heartless. And besides, if he didn't see her safely home, there was no telling what disaster would befall her and her little family.

Escorting her home was the least he could do.

"Since I have no place in particular to go, I guess I could see you home.''

"Great. It's only a couple of hours away, and when I get home I'm going to feed you a chocolate cake as big as Texas. To celebrate and to say *thank you* for rescuing Rusty.''

"Who can resist such temptation?''

The girls rode home in the car with Mandy, but she let Rusty ride on the motorcycle with Lucas. She could see them in the rearview mirror—Lucas looking like something straight out of the movies, dark and dangerous in his black jumpsuit and helmet, and Rusty looking like a carrot stuffed into the too-big helmet.

"Can I show Lucas my rock collection?'' Betsy asked.

"Of course, you can, darling.''

"Do you think he'll like it?''

"I'm sure he will. He's a nice man.''

Mandy couldn't stop smiling. Lucas was a natural with

children. Whereas Chuck had treated them as part of the price he'd paid for marriage.

The differences between the two men were mind-boggling. Lucas was caring where Chuck had been self-ish. Lucas was kind where Chuck had been scathing. Lucas was fit and trim where Chuck had gone slightly to pot.

"He's a *very* nice man," she added.

Jill popped her thumb out of her mouth long enough to ask, "Are we going to marry Lucas?"

Mandy almost ran off the road. Lucas pulled alongside her, motioning. She rolled the window down.

"Anything wrong?" he yelled.

"No." She forced a smile, then waved him off.

When he dropped back, her precocious daughter was still watching her with a disgruntled look on her face.

"Are we going to marry Lucas?" Jill repeated, as if she were conversing with a slow child.

"Of course not, Little Miss Big Britches. Whatever gave you such an idea?"

Betsy spoke up for her sister. "Rusty said you kissed him."

Mandy wanted to climb into a hole and pull the dirt in behind her. The last thing she wanted to do was con-fuse her children. Or give them the wrong idea. In fact, she didn't want to give them any ideas at all about their mother and another man. She'd worked hard to forge a secure family unit, just the four of them, plus Grandma, of course.

"Now listen, you two, we're a family and you know what that means."

"All for one and one for all," her girls chorused.

"That's right. There won't be any surprises in this family, even good ones. *We're* not going to marry *any*-

body, at least not for a long, long time. And if we do, everybody will discuss it first. Okay?''

"Okay," Jill said. Then Betsy added, "But you *kissed* Lucas, Mommy."

Even the memory made Mandy hot. She turned up the air conditioner, then fiddled with the radio till she found some nice background music to fill the pregnant silence as her girls waited for her answer.

Sometimes she wished she had the wisdom of Solomon.

"Do you remember last Halloween when Mr. Binky Blake brought us a jack-o'-lantern he'd carved?" They nodded, giggling. The pumpkin had been so big it hid everything except Mr. Blake's skinny legs and the top of his balding head. He'd looked like a walking jack-o'-lantern.

"You remember that I kissed him, too. It's a good thing to kiss our friends and let them know we appreciate the kind things they do for us."

"Like Lucas finding Rusty?" Betsy said.

"Exactly." She was relieved when the sign for Saltillo, Mississippi, came into view. "Look girls, we're almost home."

Her house was a rambling three-story white Victorian on the outskirts of the small town. It had a wraparound front porch, a three-acre yard surrounded by a fence sturdy enough to keep all her children except Rusty inside, and an ancient grove of pecan trees that bore enough nuts every fall to supply her bakery.

The house was an inheritance from Mandy's maiden Aunt Betsy Mae Bailey who had lived long enough to wear her favorite purple hat with peacock feathers to the christening of her namesake. Aunt Betsy had also willed all her furniture to Mandy, even the iron bedstead with the brass cherubs on the headboard that Mandy's mother, Evelyn, had always coveted. Evelyn considered that bequest a direct slight from her own sister, who had obviously let her talent go to her head. In her twenties and thirties, Aunt Betsy had been a singer of some note. Mandy loved her records, but was careful not to play them when her mother was around.

Her mother was standing on the front porch now, shading her eyes against the afternoon sun. When she recognized her daughter, she sat down in one of the white wicker rocking chairs on the front porch and pretended she hadn't seen them.

There was no telling what she would do when she saw Lucas Gray Wolf on his GoldWing bike. Mandy wasn't long finding out. When the bike drew to a stop beside Mandy's car, Evelyn bolted out of her rocker as if she'd been shot.

She ran down the front porch steps, completely forgetting how a woman with arthritis was supposed to walk.

When he saw her coming, Lucas took off his helmet, and Mandy waited for the inevitable scene.

"Mother, I'd like you to meet my friend Lucas." *One shock at a time,* Mandy thought, deliberately leaving off his last name. "Lucas, this is my mom, Evelyn Bailey Sullivan."

"I'm pleased to meet you, Mrs. Sullivan." Lucas's smile never wavered when Evelyn Sullivan ignored both him and his outstretched hand.

"I declare, Mandy Jean, I don't know what has gotten into you, dragging home a hoodlum on a motorcycle."

"He ain't a hoodlum," Rusty announced. "He's a real live Sioux."

"He taught me to fish," Betsy said, slipping her hand into Lucas's.

Jill poked her lower lip out. "We're going to marry him."

"Jill, shush." Mandy flushed scarlet.

"Saints preserve us." Evelyn bolted into the house, slamming the door behind her.

Lucas took everything in stride. The smile was still on his face, and he looked as if he might be suppressing laughter.

"I don't know what to say," Mandy told him. "I'm mortified. By everything."

"Your mother's refreshingly honest," Lucas said. "Most people don't have the courage."

"You're too kind."

The children lost interest in the grown-ups and raced off to the swing set under the pecan trees, while Mandy pushed her hot hair back from her face. She was torn between sending Lucas away and begging him to stay. On the one hand, it wasn't fair to subject him to the tart end of Evelyn Sullivan's tongue. On the other, it didn't seem right that the first man Mandy had been interested in since Chuck left was on the endangered list because of her mother.

"Perhaps I should just leave."

Mandy's heart stopped. At least that's what it felt like and the future stretched out in front of her, endless and lonely. The kindest thing would be to let Lucas go, but Mandy didn't feel a bit kind at the moment. She was mad as a wet hen and on fire with passion, besides.

Mandy Sullivan Belinda wasn't Irish for nothing.

"Don't you dare leave on Mother's account. It always takes her a while to get used to strangers. Once she gets to know you she'll thaw a little."

And if Lucas turned the same charm on her mother that he'd turned on her, Evelyn Sullivan would melt like a polar ice cap encountering the equator.

"I don't want to cause a problem for you."

"You won't. I can assure you."

"In that case, I'll stay."

He was watching her with that certain look, the look he'd had before he kissed her, and Mandy couldn't have moved if wild horses stampeded by. A mockingbird in a pecan tree scolded them, a trickle of sweat worked its way down her neck and into the collar of her blouse, and still Mandy stared at the man standing in her front yard.

She couldn't believe her good fortune. Lucas Gray Wolf was actually in Saltillo. There was a catch, of course. He was just passing through.

Stop, Mandy told herself. *Don't look this gift horse in the mouth.*

She wet her dry lips with the tip of her tongue. "About what Jill said—I hope you don't take it the wrong way. She's just a baby."

"Don't give it another thought," Lucas said. "I haven't."

He didn't have to be so flip about it. She, herself, had taken Jill's suggestion quite seriously. Was Lucas going to turn out to be one of those men who proclaimed they weren't the marrying kind? One of those rakes whose kisses meant nothing? One of those fly-by-night men who had a girl in every port?

She'd have him know Mandy Sullivan Belinda wasn't that kind of woman. She felt hot color rising. If she didn't get away from him she was liable to say something she would regret.

"Why don't you give me a minute with Mother?" she said.

"Certainly. I'll play with the children."

When Jill saw Lucas coming she raced toward him squealing, arms wide open. He swung her into the air, then settled her onto his hip as he bent down to hug Betsy, who was all smiles. Even Rusty looked pleased.

"Dear goodness, what have I done?" she whispered. Her children were falling in love with Lucas.

She was probably overdramatizing. Goodness knows, her mother accused her of it often enough.

"I just won't think about it right now," Mandy said aloud, then turned her back to Lucas and went into the house to talk to her mother.

Evelyn was in the kitchen cooking cornbread.

"Mother, what are you doing?"

"Cooking. I figure you brought that savage to dinner, and I'm not going to let it be said that Evelyn Sullivan ever sent a guest away hungry."

"Stop it!" Evelyn stiffened as if she'd been slapped, and Mandy moderated her tone. "Mother, you're too intelligent to act this way. Lucas Gray Wolf is one of the finest men I've ever met, and he just happens to be Native American."

"Well, I don't care if he's the Pope. I'm not wearing moccasins to the wedding."

"Good grief." Mandy sank into a kitchen chair and put her head in her hands. "This is too much."

Evelyn slammed the iron skillet into the oven. "It certainly is. I don't know what's gotten into you, Mandy Jean, marrying a man you met in the woods."

"I'm not marrying him, Mother. I just brought him to dinner."

"Why?"

"Because he saved Rusty's life." *And because I like*

him more than a little, she thought, but she wasn't about to say it to her mother.

"What are you talking about?"

"I wasn't going to tell you this, Mother, but I don't seem to have any choice."

With that, Mandy launched into the tale of the rescue. She left out the good parts, of course, the heavy breathing in the tent and the kisses in the moonlight. After she had finished, all Evelyn said was, "I'm glad I'm the kind of woman who keeps a pot roast handy."

"So am I, Mother." Mandy kissed her cheek, then took one of her famous chocolate cakes out of the freezer to thaw and went outside to find Lucas.

Chapter Four

Lucas had never gone out of his way to make anybody like him. In fact, the opposite was true. He prided himself on being a maverick and if people didn't like that, it was their tough luck.

Then why was he sitting at an antique dining table in a room decorated with wallpaper designed to give him claustrophobia, trying to be charming to a woman who obviously disliked him?

"More gravy, Lucas?" Mandy asked.

She smiled when she handed him the bowl, smiled directly into his eyes and let her hand linger on his.

And that was why Lucas was spinning the funniest tales he knew about his and Steve Thunderhorse's escapades, trying to bring a smile to Evelyn Sullivan's face. He'd failed miserably so far. Mandy's mother hadn't cracked a smile when he'd told about being cornered in

Silver Canyon by a bear that turned out to be Thunder-horse dressed in one of his Wild West Show costumes.

Maybe she didn't care for comedy. Lucas decided to try something more subtle.

"People often ask me why the ranch is named Paradise."

Evelyn didn't take the bait, but Mandy reached for his hand under the table. Hidden by the white damask table-cloth, he caressed her knuckles. She gave him a gentle squeeze of encouragement. His heart expanding and his blood pounding like war drums, Lucas turned her hand over and pressed his thumb into her palm. It was warm and slightly damp and altogether erotic. Lucas circled this thumb in that soft inviting spot. Heat spread up his arm and into his chest where it mushroomed throughout his body.

He would charm the devil for the touch of Mandy's hand.

"Tell us, Lucas," Mandy said softly. "Why is the ranch called Paradise?"

She smiled at him, and Lucas had a hard time turning away. Across the table, Evelyn pursed her lips.

Lucas turned the full force of his blue eyes on her. "My great-grandfather bought the ranch in Arizona as a place to hide. His bride had stepped in front of a train on their honeymoon, and he swore he would never love again. But Clayton Gray Wolf hadn't reckoned on a blue-eyed schoolteacher named Charity. Six days after he met her, they were married. 'At last I've found Paradise,' he said, and that's what he called the ranch."

"So that's how you got those blue eyes?" Mandy looked at him as if she might never stop, and that was fine with Lucas. In fact, with the sweet warmth of her hand still in his, it was better than fine.

It made Lucas wonder about Paradise, himself.

"Yes. That's how I got the blue eyes."

Evelyn leaned across the table, her eyes alight with the first spark of interest she'd shown since they met. "You own this Paradise Ranch?"

"Yes, I co-own it. Steve Thunderhorse is my partner."

"Where have I heard that name before?" Evelyn said.

"From the news, probably. Last Christmas, Steve married the mystery writer Angel Mercer."

"Oh, my goodness! Angel Mercer? You know Angel Mercer?"

"She and Steve live on the ranch. She's a wonderful woman."

Evelyn beamed. "The network gave their wedding nearly as much coverage as they did when Grace Kelly married her prince." She fanned herself with her napkin. "Oh my, imagine that. Angel Mercer living right on your ranch."

Mandy squeezed his hand, then leaned over to whisper, "Bingo."

"What was that, Mandy?" Evelyn said. "What did you say?"

"I asked Lucas if he likes bing cherries. I think I'll put some on top of the chocolate cake."

"I love bing cherries," he said.

"Good. I'll be right back."

Her leg brushed his when she left the table. Was it deliberate? Lucas hoped so. Smiling broadly, he leaned slightly toward Evelyn as she peppered him with questions about Angel.

"I've read every one of her books, even the early ones about that cat," Evelyn said. "Do you think she'd autograph them if I sent them home by you?"

"I think she would. I'll be happy to try."

"Now, tell me again about how you rescued my grand-son. Mandy's told me once, but I want to hear every last detail from you."

"Aw, Grandma," Rusty said.

"Now, you shush up, young man. I want to get the story straight."

Rusty grimaced. "That means she's gonna gossip to everybody at the beauty parlor."

"Mind your manners, young man. Talking about a family hero is *not* gossip."

Lucas sat back, satisfied. In the course of one evening he'd gone from hoodlum to hero.

Mission accomplished, he thought, and all for the sake of Mandy, who appeared in the doorway looking flushed and beautiful, a tiny dab of chocolate at the corner of her mouth.

She'd been stealing a taste of chocolate as if she couldn't wait to have something so decadently delicious in her mouth. Lucas's passion stirred so strongly that he was glad the tablecloth covered his lap.

"Chocolate cake, anyone?" Mandy asked, and her children erupted into a chorus of *yes*es, which quickly turned into an argument over who got the biggest piece.

Lucas was watching her, a lone wolf in the midst of merry mayhem. She wished she knew what he was think-ing. Did he feel trapped, anxious to leave? Was he smil-ing merely to be polite?

"I apologize for all this madness," she said to him.

"No problem. In fact, I'm enjoying it. I missed all this growing up."

Her heart ached for the little orphaned boy, and she brushed her hand lightly across his to say, *I care.* He smiled directly into her eyes, and if Jill hadn't spilled cake on the floor, Mandy might have made a fool of herself in front of her mother.

"I'll help clean that up," Lucas said.

Evelyn jumped up from the table, as spry as a sixteen year old. "Nonsense. I'm going to take care of everything, and the children will help me. The two of you are going to the front porch to sit on the swing."

"There's no need for that, Mother."

"Indeed, there is. Mr. Gray Wolf is our guest. I won't have him doing chores."

"Call me Lucas, please."

Evelyn beamed at him. "Lucas, it'll soon be dark and the moon vine will be blooming. Mandy's daddy proposed to me by the moon vine. It's very romantic."

Flushed and giddy, Mandy led the way to the front porch. A breeze had sprung up and set the wind chimes tinkling. With her back to Lucas, Mandy leaned against a white column and lifted her hair to the cooling breeze.

Goose bumps rose on her skin. He was watching her.

"Subtlety is not Mother's style," she said. "I hope you don't take this the wrong way."

Silence. Hadn't he heard? What was he thinking? His footsteps sounded like drum beats as he crossed the plank flooring. Then he was standing behind her, so close his pant leg brushed the back of her thigh.

"What would the wrong way be, Mandy?"

"Oh, you know." She didn't dare turn around, for she'd never been able to hide her feelings. He would see naked longing.

"No, I don't." He bracketed her shoulders, and she shivered with pure delight. If she could feel his hands on her for the next hundred years, she'd be happy. "Tell me, Mandy."

"Well, that remark about romance, for instance.

Mother was off base as well as out of line. I'm not the least bit interested in a relationship, and I'm sure you're not, either.''

Oh, dear heavens. Would he think she was fishing? She was making a total mess of things.

"Not that it's any of my business," she said, blundering on. "I mean, what you do is strictly your business, but as for me, well, taking care of a family is a full-time occupation. Of course, you can see that without me having to point it out."

Why was he so quiet? And why were his hands still on her? Not that she minded. No, indeed.

"What I mean is, romance is just not part of my agenda."

Why in the world didn't he say something? Do something?

"Speak for yourself, Mandy."

His voice was deep and rich and sexy, and when his lips touched the back of her neck she thought she'd died and gone to heaven. His touch was that powerful, that wonderful.

Good heavens. She could eat this man with a spoon.

He brushed his lips across her skin once more. In view of her staunch proclamation about a romanticless agenda, she felt called upon to say something witty and sophisticated.

"Oh my," she whispered. And then she sighed. Mandy and sophistication had never even been on speaking terms.

Slowly, he turned her around and pulled her into his arms. Then he cupped her chin, tipped her face up and kissed the corner of her mouth.

"Hmmm, delicious," he said. "Chocolate. It's my favorite."

"Chocolate?"

"Yes. You had a little smudge in the corner of your mouth when you came out of the kitchen with the cake."

"Oh, well, I couldn't resist."

"Neither could I. I've been wanting to do that all evening."

She'd been wanting him to do that, and more. But still valiantly struggling for sophistication, she didn't tell him so.

"Would you like to see the moon vine?" she asked.

"Only if you promise it will be romantic."

Wouldn't it be wonderful if he were serious? "I never make promises I can't keep. All I can tell you is that it's spectacularly beautiful and intensely fragrant."

"Sounds awfully romantic to me."

"You don't strike me as the sentimental type."

"How *do* I strike you, Mandy?"

With lighting bolts and star showers and Fourth of July fireworks, she thought.

"Oh, I don't know." His hand was still on her chin, and they were standing so close she was afraid she'd ignite and go up in flames any minute now. "A wanderer. A maverick. A lone wolf."

"I've been called all those things, and more." He tucked her hand through his arm. "Show me this remarkable vine, Mandy."

"We don't have far to go."

"I'm disappointed. I'd hoped to go to the moon with you."

Was he teasing her? She glanced up to see his eyes sparkling with mischief. He was.

She led him the length of the porch and around the corner where a sweet fragrance enveloped them.

"There," she said. "Over the railing behind the swing. That's the moon vine."

Trumpet-shaped flowers glowed in the darkness, huge and milky white, and shining down on them was a moon as big as her Grandma Bailey's washtub.

"It's spectacular," Lucas said. "And very evocative."

Magic rarely happened in Mandy's life, but when it did, it struck with such force that she was dumbfounded. Suddenly she saw the moment for what it was, a magical gift, and she wasn't about to waste a minute of it.

"Come." She tugged at his arm. "I want to show you a special place where the moon flowers are so big they look like flying saucers."

Her special place was deep in the woods beside the house, far away from the glow of lighted windows and the gleam of prying eyes. The gazebo rose out of the midst of the trees like a Victorian lady bedecked for her wedding day. It was painted the purest white, and sprouting from the lattices were giant blossoms of such intense sweetness the air tasted like honey.

Closing her eyes, Mandy breathed in the nectar. When Lucas lifted her off her feet, she didn't utter a single protest. And when he carried her into that flower-laden bower and lowered her feet to the floor without losing one iota of body contact, she didn't make a declaration of independence. Not one.

"I hope your intentions are strictly dishonorable," she whispered.

"On the contrary. My intentions are strictly romantic."

His kiss literally took her breath away. When her feet left the floor she would swear they had wings. Lucas was holding her up, of course, but she was too busy to get bogged down in mundane details. For one thing, her heart took flight, and then she heard bells in the hills and music, to boot. Suddenly Mandy was the star of her own Broadway show, and every trite phrase she'd ever heard came true.

And all because Lucas was kissing her.

What do you think you're doing? The brief warning echoed through Lucas's mind, but he pushed it aside. Mandy was made to be kissed, and he was kissing her. It was that simple.

Wasn't it?

He loved the taste of her lips, the shape of her body molded against his, the soft murmuring sounds of pleasure she made. He loved that she'd disclaimed any interest in the sentimental, and then had brought him to the most romantic spot on her home property.

Lucas was a hopeless romantic, but always about other people's affairs. Tonight, he was making an exception. The moon was full, the flowers were fragrant, and the woman was willing. Besides that, she'd clearly stated that she had no interest in a relationship. In essence, she'd given him the green light to enjoy the moment, and then, when the time came, to walk away with a clear conscience.

Hadn't she?

He came up for air, and she murmured, "Hmm. I love kissing...you."

And so he kissed her again. Fire raced along the surface of his skin, and his blood roared like a raging river.

He tightened his hold. She was deliciously soft and feminine, warm, ripe, erotic. Did she know how much he wanted her? How could she not? His body kept no secrets.

Another time, another place, he'd have lowered her to the floor and satisfied his longings. But her house was too close by, and in it were her mother and her children.

Deep down, he knew Mandy was not the kind of woman to give in to illicit primitive urges in the bosom of her family.

Raging with a passion so intense it burned his bones, Lucas devoured her lips, taking every ounce of sweetness she had to offer. She flowered open for him and took his tongue deep into the hot inner recesses of her mouth, all the while making those erotic sounds that hummed through Lucas with the insistence of war drums.

He was almost over the brink when she pulled back.

"Lucas." She bracketed his face with her hands. "Oh, Lucas."

"You are so sweet," he said.

"No. No, I'm not. I'm greedy. And selfish to the bone."

"I don't believe a word of that."

"Yes, I am. I invited you here for this." She traced his lips with the tips of her fingers. "Just for this."

"I thought I came for chocolate cake," he said, hoping to tease her out of her self-incriminating mood.

"Oh, you." She swatted him on the arm, laughing. Then she moved away, sat down on the bench that circled the inside of the gazebo and wrapped her arms around herself. "You don't mind that I used you?"

He wanted to sit beside her and offer comfort and reassurance and a strong shoulder to lean on. Common sense and a healthy aversion to attachments stopped him.

"That makes us even," he said. "I'm using you, too."

"Oh." She put her hand to her mouth, and her eyes were deep, bottomless green pools. A man could drown in them. "Well…good," she murmured.

The moon cast a silver shadow over her. She looked soft, fragile, breakable. *Careful,* something inside Lucas warned. The last thing he wanted to do was break her.

"Then, you don't mind that I'm going to ask you to stay?"

She had such a little-girl-lost quality, he wanted to kiss her again. But if he started, he might never stop.

"No, I don't mind. Ask me."

"Will you stay? At least for the night?"

The thought of being cooped up inside four walls gave him pause. Mandy mistook his silence.

"I'll understand, of course, if you say no." She pushed her hair away from her flushed face, a gesture that was becoming increasingly familiar to him, and very endearing. "After all, we've been nothing but a pack of trouble for you..."

"Mandy..."

"And I *do* understand how much you want to get on the road..."

"Mandy..." Squatting in front of her, Lucas put his fingers on her lips. "Shh. Listen to me. Are you listening?" She nodded, her eyes as round and shining as silver dollars. "I *want* to stay."

"You don't mind being in a house?"

"I'll open the windows."

"You'll be upstairs on the second floor."

"I'll hang a bedsheet out the window in case of emergencies." He grinned, loving how she looked when he teased her, her face flushed and glowing.

"Mother sleeps downstairs and the children sleep on the third floor." Her blush deepened. "I hope you don't think I'm suggesting anything...improper."

"The thought never entered my mind." He kissed her hand. "Mandy, I can assure you that I will conduct myself like a gentleman. For once in my life."

"I have no complaints."

"Good. It's settled then. I'll sleep in a real bed on the

second floor with the windows open and the pleasant knowledge that you'll be just down the hall.'' The smile that bloomed across her face was one of genuine relief. "You will be down the hall, won't you, Mandy?"

"Yes. I'll be down the hall, Lucas. You can call if you need me. I mean, if you need an extra blanket or anything."

"Relax, Mandy." He patted her hand. "I know you're a lady."

She sighed. "Sometimes, Lucas, I wish I weren't."

Lucas's bedroom was high-ceilinged and spacious, with a wide bank of windows along the east wall. He immediately flung open the windows and checked the lay of the land. Looking for escape routes, his heart beat a quick tattoo. In spite of the flip tone he'd used with Mandy, he carefully noted that in case of fire he could reach the branches of the big oak tree outside his window.

Breathing a sigh of relief, Lucas sat down to take off his boots. Upstairs, Mandy was moving around in her children's rooms, tucking them in for the night. He could hear her footsteps on the floorboards.

Jill had whined for Lucas to read a good-night story, but Mandy had quickly put a stop to it. Lucas was both relieved and somewhat saddened. He had actually wanted to go upstairs and be a part of the children's bedtime routine. He'd wanted to read them a story, to pull the covers under Betsy's chin, to kiss Jill's downy cheek. He'd wanted to feel the warm glow of being an intimate part of Mandy's family.

On the other hand, he'd wanted to escape to the solitude of a room far away from the magnetic pull of three dependent, fatherless children…and their incredibly appealing mother.

He heard Mandy's soft footfalls coming down the staircase, and when he found himself holding his breath waiting for her to come into his room, he knew he was in trouble. He let out a long sigh when she passed on by.

What had he expected? That she'd tuck him in, too?

He stripped off his shirt and hung it over the back of a rocking chair. The cushion was ruby-colored velvet and very old. Lucas ran his hand over the fabric. Her mother had probably rocked her in that chair. Or perhaps even her grandmother.

Mandy lived in a house full of furniture that had probably been handed down to her through generations of family. She was surrounded by objects that had meaning in her life. She had stability, a home, a family, a place in the community.

There was no place in her life for a rancher with war paint in his blood and wanderlust in his heart. Then why was he suddenly hurrying down the hall toward her room?

To say goodnight, he told himself. Merely to say goodnight.

She hadn't heard him coming. Lucas liked to think it was because of the stealth that was a part of his Sioux heritage, though it could just as easily have been that he'd forgotten his shoes as well as his shirt.

Mandy stood at the window brushing her hair, her back to the door, her body silhouetted by the moonlight. She was starlight and moonbeam, fantasy and dream, and yet she was vividly alive, genuine and real, flesh and blood and bone arranged in a manner that stole his breath.

Leaning against the door frame he watched her in secret, memorizing the curve of her arm as she stroked the brush through her shining hair, the arch of her neck, the thrust of her breasts, full and lush against the gauzy fabric of her dressing gown. Her image burned into his mind, and he knew if he lived to be a hundred and ten he would never forget the sight of Mandy standing in her moon-washed bedroom brushing her hair.

She turned toward him slowly, her lips softly parted, her brush poised in midair. Had he made a sound, whispered her name, or had the force of his longing been enough to alert her to his presence?

"Lucas?"

"I just stopped by to say good-night."

"Oh." She started to run the brush through her hair once more, then she stopped, suddenly aware of her attire. "I'm not dressed."

"Neither am I." The moon burnished his naked chest as he moved toward her. He heard her sharp intake of breath, saw the widening of her eyes. "Don't be afraid."

"I'm not. I could never be afraid of you, Lucas."

"Good."

He was so close now he could smell her sweet fragrance, see the burst of gold in the center of her eyes. She drew a sharp breath, then ran the tip of her tongue over her lips. They were full and still slightly puffy from where he'd kissed them.

Lucas wanted to do it again. And more, ever so much more.

Reigning in his passion, he took the brush from her and slowly began to stroke her hair.

"You are so beautiful," he whispered. "So very beautiful."

"No man has ever said that to me."

"Then they've all been fools."

He followed the shining path of the brush with his

hand. Red-gold curls clung to his fingers, soft and silky. Lucas pressed his lips to her hair.

Sighing, she leaned into him. "I wish I were the kind of woman who could ask you to stay. Here. In my bedroom."

"I'm the kind of man who doesn't need an invitation."

"Ohh."

"Usually."

He continued stroking her hair, partly because he loved the intimacy of it, partly to keep his hands occupied with something more innocent than what he was longing to do.

"That feels so good," she whispered.

Her gown floated in the breeze stirred by the ceiling fan, touching his pant leg.

"Yes, it does."

The brush was his surrogate, sliding, stroking in a slow, smooth rhythm that set his heart on fire.

"Lucas?"

"Yes?"

"I'm so glad it was you who found Rusty in the woods."

"So am I."

Setting the brush on the windowsill, he buried his fingers in her hair and lifted it off her neck. Then leaning down he pressed hot kisses on the slender, silvery column.

"Lucas?"

"Hmm?"

"I wish this didn't ever have to stop."

Say the word and it won't, he wanted to say, but Mandy was so vulnerable. Innocent, somehow.

"You're a lady, remember? And I'm a gentleman. At least, for the evening."

He turned her around and tipped up her chin, but when he saw her face he forgot what he had been going to say. Tears sparkled in her eyes and clung to the ends of her lashes.

"I'm so silly," she whispered.

"You're not silly. You're warm and real and wonderful."

"Sometimes it's so hard, wanting the things you know you can't have."

A great battle raged through Lucas, with his better half striving to tell Mandy he'd give her everything she ever wanted, and his dark half telling him to run like the wind and never look back. Never.

Lucas struck a compromise.

"Goodnight, Mandy." He placed a chaste kiss on her lips. "Sweet dreams."

"You too, Lucas." Her fingertips brushed across his chest, light and cool as the kiss of snowflakes.

He didn't make a sound when he left her room. And he didn't look back.

He didn't dare.

Chapter Five

Lucas knew he couldn't stay in that house one more night. Not because of the four walls that seemed to close around him, but because of the woman down the hall. Mandy in her diaphanous gown. Mandy with her luscious body. Mandy with her silky hair and glowing skin.

Mandy. She was too tempting. Having her so close by and yet completely out of his reach was exquisite torture.

Lucas left the bed he wasn't sleeping in anyhow, and stood beside the window, gazing at the moon. He couldn't stay, and yet he couldn't leave.

He'd promised to teach Rusty how to carve a whistle. And that would take time. Wouldn't it?

He was fooling himself, of course. There was one reason for staying, and her name was Mandy.

A star plummeted, leaving a silvery trail across the night sky. Lucas believed in omens. Standing at the window, he pondered the message of the star until he was so sleepy he could finally lie between the sheets and close his eyes, if not in peace, then in pleasant exhaustion.

Mandy was always the first one up, which didn't present a problem at all today since she'd been up most of the night anyhow. How could any woman in her right mind sleep after seeing Lucas Gray Wolf's naked chest in the moonlight? If the upper half of him was that gorgeous, what would the rest of him be like?

She couldn't believe she'd had the audacity to run her hands over his chest. The problem was, she wished she'd done more.

Sighing, she pulled her pink terry-cloth robe over her gown. Women with three children upstairs and a mother downstairs didn't do more; they did less. They acted sensible and kept their distance, emotional as well as real. Which is exactly what she was going to do, starting today.

Nevertheless, she brushed her hair with unusual care and put on her most flattering pink lipstick before heading to the kitchen.

Mandy tiptoed on the stairs and carefully avoided stepping in the middle of the third step from the bottom so it wouldn't squeak. When she got to the bottom she smelled coffee.

"Mother?" she called, hurrying toward the kitchen.

"No. Lucas." Leaning against the cabinets in jeans and a faded T-shirt with a cup of coffee in his hand, he was perfectly glorious. A masculine presence that overwhelmed her in a delicious way.

"I hope you don't mind," he said.

"Mind? Why, I think you're the sexiest thing I've ever seen in my kitchen." She turned red to the roots of her hair, and his eyes gleamed with merriment, but he didn't laugh. And that was her saving grace. Mandy plopped into a chair and propped her chin in her hand. "Good grief. You're going to think I'm a country bumpkin."

"On the contrary. I think you're the most refreshing woman I've met in a long time."

It could have been worse. He could have said, *the nicest,* which was about the most noncommittal a man could be.

Mandy would settle for refreshing.

Lucas handed her a cup of steaming coffee and sat beside her. Close enough so that his thigh bumped against hers. Was it deliberate? She hoped so.

"I hope you don't mind," he said.

"Mind? No, not at all. There's no reason for you to sit on the other side."

"About the coffee, I mean."

"Well, of course not. That's what I mean, too." Mandy became an accomplished liar on the spot. The next thing she knew she'd be taking up other bad habits, such as outrageous flirting and outright seduction. "Sitting on the other side of this big table would be like sharing a cup of coffee with a stranger in the next county."

Lucas let her remark go unchallenged, proving himself to be a true gentleman.

"I don't want to be a stranger," he said.

He pressed closer, his leg in full contact with hers. Mandy forgot to breathe. And when he captured her in one of those piercing blue-eyed stares, her heart forgot to beat.

Mandy was drowning, drowning. He was so close, and yet so far away. She wished she had the courage to rip aside her sensible terry-cloth robe and offer herself to him. More than that, she wished she'd had the audacity to come to the kitchen in the green silk teddy she'd been saving for a special occasion. Green for go. She wouldn't even have to make an offer.

The air was thick with longing. Mostly hers, she guessed, but the way he was looking at her, some of it might be his, too. She hoped so.

"Mandy..."

He leaned close. She thought he was going to kiss her, and she knew if he did she would never be able to stop kissing him back. Among other things.

The sunrise was changing from the first faint blush that she loved to a golden glow that would have her entire family trooping down the stairs in fifteen minutes. Fifteen minutes was not long enough to do all the things she wanted to do with Lucas Gray Wolf.

Mandy wet her lips with the tip of her tongue. "I didn't hear you come down the stairs this morning," she whispered.

"I always get up early. I hope I didn't wake you."

"No. I wasn't sleeping."

"Neither was I."

She bloomed at his confession, bloomed and was made bold.

"Was it because you were inside a house?"

"Yes." The air between them was charged. He was so close now their lips were almost touching. "Because I was in your house, Mandy."

"Oh..." His warm breath stirred against her face. Mandy closed her eyes and tried to inhale him.

"Did you see the shooting star, Mandy?"

"Yes," she whispered. Lucas was a winter coat that she could wear whenever she wanted to be warm and cozy. With her eyes still closed she could feel him on her skin, heating her up all the way to her bones.

"It was a sign—" he cupped her face, his hands as

gentle as the wings of a summer monarch on sweet
creamy phlox ''—a sign that we're supposed to be together.''

If she opened her eyes, would she find out she was
dreaming? Mandy kept them tightly shut. She had had
enough shattered dreams to last a lifetime.

''Mandy, open your eyes and look at me.'' Did she
dare? Lucas caressed her cheeks, murmuring, ''Mandy,
Mandy.''

The sun seemed to be rising on his face. ''If I asked
you to go away with me, would you?'' Mandy blinked.
This couldn't be happening to her. Dreams only came
true in fairy tales.

''Just for a little while,'' he said. ''A few days. The
two of us. Alone. Together.''

What would her mother say? What would the neighbors say? What would she tell her children?

*I'm going off with this gorgeous man who is offering
me nothing but a few days of pleasure because I can't
bear the thought of never having known him intimately?
Just once I'm doing something reckless because it feels
good? I want to have something wonderful to remember
the rest of my life?*

''Yes,'' she said, not because she was that kind of
woman, but because she wasn't.

Just this once she was going to be a dauntless, adven-
turous kind of woman. And when she came home she'd
have enough memories to last a lifetime.

''I'll go with you, Lucas.''

Lucas never had second thoughts. Once he made up
his mind about something, he didn't look back. Good or
bad, his decisions stood.

Today was an exception. He was sitting on the front

porch steps with Rusty, teaching him how to carve a whistle, and somewhere in the house Mandy was breaking the news to her mother. The news about Lucas's invitation. The invitation that now loomed in his mind as one of the most foolhardy things he'd ever done.

He didn't have to wonder what had possessed him to ask her into the woods. It was passion, plain and simple. A primitive lust that had taken hold of him and wouldn't let go.

"Don't cut too deep, Rusty, or you'll ruin the whistle."

"You've already told me that twice, Lucas."

"That's something you can't hear too often, Rusty. You want to be a good wood carver, don't you?"

"Yeah."

"Then pay attention."

In addition to becoming foolhardy, he'd also become adept at obfuscation. And all because of Mandy.

"I could say the same thing to you. I bet you've looked in that window fifty times. What's so all-fired important in the house?"

"Nothing." If Lucas were Pinocchio, his nose would be fifteen feet long.

The woman in that house was far more important to him than she should be. And that's what was giving him pause. His plan was for the two of them to go off for a few days and get all this pent-up ardor out of their systems. Then he would go his way and she would go hers.

Why, all of a sudden, was Lucas so certain it wouldn't work that way? Why was he on the verge of running into the house and saying, "Forget what I said, I take it all back"?

It wouldn't take five minutes, and then he could be on his way.

Inside, Mandy passed by the window, her face shining like Christmas lights. Lucas liked to think he was the reason. She viewed him as some kind of hero, and he was beginning to get used to the idea. More than get used to it. He was beginning to like it.

"After we carve this whistle, do you have time to show me how to make a slingshot?"

"Sure thing, Rusty."

Lucas had all the time in the world.

Mandy seldom beat around the bush, but that's what she had been doing with her mother for the last fifteen minutes. She'd started the conversation in the den where she thought her mother would be most comfortable. Evelyn was always in a better mood when she was comfortable.

Mandy's opening gambit had been, "I think it's important for people to take time off for themselves," which had led Evelyn into a five-minute monologue about the maiden sisters, Janet and Matilda Crump, whose last trip to Europe had turned into a six-month sojourn abroad that had brought them all kinds of excitement, including a proposal of marriage to Janet by a man twenty-five years her junior.

"Imagine that, at her age. Thinking a fifty-year-old man would look twice at an old fossil like her. If you ask me, what he was looking at was her money. Everybody knows Matthew Crump made a killing in the stock market."

When her mother had stopped for breath, Mandy had maneuvered her into her domain, the kitchen. Put Mandy in a room with copper-bottomed pots and stainless-steel pans, and she positively shone. Usually.

Unfortunately, today was not usual. If it hadn't been

for her daughters' squeals of laughter floating down the stairs, Mandy would have felt like a wanderer lost on another planet. That's how alien her plan felt to her. Imagine what it would seem like to her mother.

Mandy sighed.

"What's the matter, Mandy? You seem distracted."

"I guess you could say that, Mother."

"Would it have anything to do with that handsome man sitting out yonder on the front porch with Rusty?" Evelyn's smile was coy.

"As a matter of fact, it does."

"Are you going to tell me, or are you going to drag me all over this house trying to work up your courage?"

"I guess there's only one way to say this, and that's to come right out and tell the truth."

"He proposed!" Evelyn clapped her hands. "I knew he would. I didn't tell him about that moon vine for nothing, no sirree. Evelyn Bailey Sullivan wasn't born yesterday."

"Mother…"

Fluffing up her hair, Evelyn rattled on. "I do know my way around a man, if I do say so myself. Why, in my day…"

"Mother!"

"What's the matter with you? A woman can be proud of a son-in-law like that. Yes sirree, I knew the first time I laid eyes on him, Lucas was a man of character."

"I believe you called him a hoodlum."

"Pshaw. That's just my way of testing a man's mettle, seeing what he's made of." Evelyn made a beeline for the kitchen phone.

"What are you doing?"

"Calling Joyce. I can't wait to tell her." Evelyn started to dial.

"Mother, I'm not getting married."

Evelyn stopped in mid-dial. "You turned him down?"

"He didn't propose."

"Well, why not, I'd like to know? The two of you get along famously. Don't tell me he's the kind of man who believes in long courtships. Why, your father proposed to me practically the second he met me."

The whole thing was getting out of hand. Why had she ever thought she could go off with Lucas?

"Lucas asked me to go away with him for a few days, that's all."

Quietly, Evelyn cradled the phone, then sat down at the kitchen table, staring at her daughter.

"Well, why didn't you say so in the first place?"

"You're not...upset?"

"I think *shock* is the word you're casting about for. No, I'm not shocked. Believe it or not, your mother's intelligent enough to realize that people do things differently these days."

"That's beside the point now. I'm not going. I don't know why I ever thought I could. I have responsibilities."

"You most certainly are, young lady. You know perfectly well I'm capable of taking care of the children. These opportunities come along once in a blue moon. You go with that handsome man. It'll be a sort of honeymoon before the wedding."

"Mother, please put marriage out of your mind. It's not that kind of trip."

"How do you know?"

"Because Lucas is not the marrying kind, and I'm an independent woman." He was, wasn't he? And she was, wasn't she? Suddenly, Mandy was sure of only one thing:

she was going with Lucas even if it turned the whole town upside down.

Evelyn pursed her lips, thinking. Then she polished her glasses, a signal that she planned to dispense advice and required undivided attention.

"Mandy, did I ever tell you about the time when I was eight and my brother and I brought home a squirrel with a broken leg?"

"I don't think so."

"Daddy told me wild animals didn't make good pets and Josh and I could keep him only till his leg got well. That squirrel stayed ten years. When he died, it was like we'd lost a member of the family."

"Lucas is not a squirrel," Mandy said, but still, Lucas did put her in mind of something wild, something deliciously untamed.

"The point is, Mandy, you never know what will happen. All I'm saying is don't rule out any possibilities."

"I'm not ruling anything out, Mother. I just don't want anybody clinging to any false illusions."

"He's a mighty fine prospect, and Lord knows, they are few and far between in this town."

"I wish you wouldn't think of Lucas that way, Mother. And I certainly don't want the children to get their hopes built up. They already like him too much."

"What will you tell your children, Mandy?"

"Only that I'm taking a vacation. That's all it is, and that's all they need to know. Lucas is leaving tonight after supper. He'll pick me up in the morning at the shop."

"All right, Mandy, have it your way." Evelyn adjusted her glasses and gave her daughter one of those long, pregnant looks she was famous for. Over the years, Mandy had learned to endure that kind of scrutiny with equanimity. "All I'm saying is, be careful that you don't get more than you bargained for."

The minute Lucas saw Mandy's shop, he knew he'd made another mistake. He'd made it a practice to keep his distance from the women who passed briefly through his life. He didn't want to know their families, he didn't want to see their homes, he didn't want to see their workplaces.

First, he'd taken Mandy's children under his wing; then, he'd stayed in her house, and now this.

The shop was as charming as the woman who owned it. A renovated hardware store in a late nineteenth-century building, it had ivy climbing the weathered brick walls, a green awning over the door, and a stained-glass panel featuring doves and ribbons and flowers above the enormous display window. The cakes and cookies and pies arrayed there invited him to press his nose against the window.

That's exactly what he did, and that's how Mandy found him.

She must have entered through the back, for suddenly she appeared in a doorway just beyond the display window. Lucas found himself staring at Mandy over a three-layer wedding cake with sugar bells on the top.

Her smile bloomed on a face already so radiant she reminded him of pictures he'd seen of brides in the social section of the newspaper. She hurried across her shop, and when she appeared at the front door, she was breathless.

"Everything looks good enough to eat," he said.

He loved it when she blushed. He loved that she took his statement personally.

"So do you." Realizing what she'd said, her hands flew to her hot cheeks. "Oh my."

He laughed with sheer delight. Then, so she wouldn't misunderstand, he said, "I love your spontaneous quality, Lady. Don't ever lose it."

"That's unlikely. Mother calls it putting your foot in your mouth. Why did you call me 'Lady'?"

"Because you are."

"Would you like a tour of the shop?"

Beyond the display cases, he caught a glimpse of the kitchen, all polished pans and gleaming surfaces. Two women swathed in white aprons were pounding enormous mounds of dough.

Lucas had the feeling that if he stepped through the doorway he would become even further embroiled in Mandy's life, like a wasp caught in a spider's web. Everywhere he turned, the threads were wrapping him tighter.

"Some other time, perhaps. I really would like to get on the road. Are you ready?"

"I've never been more ready in my life." Her blush deepened, and she bit her lower lip. "I'm afraid I'm not very good at this. I mean, this is not the sort of thing I do every day, or *any* day, for that matter."

Another silken strand wound itself around Lucas, this time in the vicinity of his heart. He took her hand.

"Mandy, you can say *no* at any time, and there will be no hard feelings. I want you to understand that. I don't want you to do anything that makes you uncomfortable in any way. I don't want you to do anything you will regret."

"I don't plan to say *no,* Lucas, not now and not later."

Her honest declaration stirred him in ways he'd never thought possible. It stirred his body, his heart, his imagination. If he had been one of his ancestors, he'd have laid a buffalo robe at her feet. He'd have brought her a painted pony that would carry her like the wind and a necklace of green glass beads that would match her eyes. He would have carried her into his tepee and covered her with a blanket woven with red and yellow and blue and purple, and there underneath the rainbow of colors he would have made her his own.

But he was a modern Sioux, bearing nothing more than a scruffy old backpack, and so he gave her the only gift he had—the gift of song. Spreading his blue jean jacket on the sidewalk, he took her arm and escorted her to his GoldWing bike, all the while singing "On the Sunny Side of the Street."

As he fitted her into the helmet and jumpsuit and stowed her belongings, her laughter pealed on the summer air. He tossed his jacket into his knapsack, then steadied the bike and winked at her.

"Going my way, Lady?"

"It just so happens I am, Mr. Gray Wolf."

She mounted behind him, and they roared off down the street.

Chapter Six

The bike roared beneath her like something alive, and the landscape whizzed by at a dizzying speed. Panicked and exhilarated at the same time, Mandy suddenly felt displaced. Surely this was not staid, sensible Mandy Belinda racing down the road on this monstrous contraption. Surely this was not Mandy Belinda, mother of three, with her arms wrapped around a handsome stranger heading blithely into the woods with the intent of exploring more than the flora and the fauna. Some other woman had climbed into her skin. That had to be it. Some other woman who planned to do wickedly delicious things.

Her helmet was equipped with a radio hookup so that she could hear both the music and Lucas. His voice came to her now, disembodied but comforting.

"How are you doing back there, Mandy?"

"Great."

"I'm not scaring you, am I? If I am, I'll slow down a little."

"No. I'm fine. Really, I am."

How fast were they going? Mandy didn't dare look, didn't dare ask.

"There's a steep curve coming up, Mandy. Remember to sit very still. If you lean, be sure it's in the same direction I'm leaning."

She tightened her hold and concentrated on sitting perfectly upright. When the big bike leaned into the curve, the ground came alarmingly close. Mandy shut her eyes.

"You're doing just fine, Mandy."

"That part was easy."

The part that wouldn't be easy was coming up—the part where the sun went down and Lucas spread a sleeping bag that was probably big enough for both of them if they slept really close. She hadn't slept with a man in a long time. What if she snored? Of course, snoring wasn't really what was bothering Mandy. It was everything that led up to the snoring.

They stopped for dinner at a mom-and-pop place with whitewashed walls, green shutters and a screen door that popped shut behind them. The sign out front said "Eat."

"I love places like this," Lucas said, shedding his helmet and jumpsuit, then helping Mandy out of hers. "No pretense, no fuss, just plain good food served in simple surroundings by friendly people."

Mandy didn't reply right away. She stood quietly, surveying her surroundings.

Lucas wondered if he'd made a mistake. What if Mandy were the kind of woman who liked fancy places with linen napkins and real silverware? What if she were the kind who disdained places like this? The kind who found fault with him for not spending more money on her?

He heard Mandy sigh. Was that a good sign or a bad one? Lucas could face a herd of wild ponies and never blink an eye, but in this small Tennessee town that didn't even have a traffic light, he was suddenly as uncertain and nervous as a teenager on his first date.

"We can go somewhere else if you like," he said.

He was already reaching for his helmet when Mandy put her hand on his arm.

"I love this place. Really, I do."

Her smile was the only affirmation he needed. He led her to a corner table that sported a yellow plastic cloth decorated with blue daisies. Mandy traced the pattern and he noticed that her fingernails were squared off and natural, no polish, no glitter. He liked that.

"My granddaddy Sullivan used to own a place very much like this," she said. "I remember going there after school and on Saturdays so I could watch him cook. He made the best fried peach pies in two counties."

"Is that where you learned to cook?"

"Yes. Not only did I learn to cook from Granddaddy Sullivan, I learned to love cooking. He always sang, blues for soups and stews that cooked slowly, Broadway show tunes for anything that required dough, and hymns for the meat."

"Why hymns for the meat?"

"He said that's what he was always most grateful for, that he had enough money to buy the best cuts of rump roast."

"He must be quite a character."

"He was. A tornado destroyed it all—Granddaddy, Grandma, and the store."

A woman in blue jeans and a pink sweatshirt that said

"Kissing won't last but good cooking will" came to take their order. She introduced herself as Mureen.

"Pronounced just like the eyedrops," she said. When she smiled she showed a gold tooth at the front. "I suggest the house speciality, especially since it's the *only* speciality."

"And what is that?" Lucas asked.

"Corned beef and cabbage picked fresh this morning out of my own garden. Top it off with cherry pie and some of Granny's good homemade vanilla ice cream and you'll leave here smiling. That's for sure."

Lucas ordered two of everything.

Lucas settled back to watch Mandy eat. It was a luxury he hadn't allowed himself at her house, partly because her family might notice and partly because of his training. The housemother in the orphanage had told him it wasn't polite to stare. At the time he'd been watching Kitsy Davis consume moon pies and wondering whether the marshmallows caused her to blow up so big.

He watched Mandy for another reason. Lucas believed a woman's sexual appetite was inextricably linked to her enjoyment of food. Not the amount consumed, but the amount of appreciation for differences in taste and texture.

Thunderhorse called it a half-baked theory, but Lucas had countered that, over the years, he'd never known it to fail.

One bite of cabbage, and Mandy murmured, "Mmm, delicious." A bite of the corned beef and she closed her eyes in ecstasy. She passed the homebaked bread under her nose, then pronounced the aroma *heavenly*.

Lucas couldn't stop smiling. Here was a woman who used all her senses to enhance her enjoyment of a meal.

What would she do with the homemade ice cream?
More to the point, what would she do under the moonlight when he spread kisses over her thighs?

He could hardly wait to find out.

They had pitched camp beside the Tennessee River in
a beautiful spot that Mandy thought of as a mossy glen.
Or perhaps a secret garden. Ancient oak trees, under-
grown with muscadine and blackberry vines, provided a
thick shield of privacy, while honeysuckle and the tiny
star-like flowers from the sweet bay magnolia perfumed
the air. The fragrance reminded Mandy of the sugar-
cinnamon topping she used on her shortbread cookies,
sweet and spicy. A seductive aroma.

Thinking of the green silk teddy she'd tucked among
her things, Mandy was suddenly shy. Here was a man
she desired more than any man she'd ever known, and
she didn't have the first inkling what to do about it.

Or, for that matter, what he would do. She'd been too
long married, too long out of the loop.

Lucas had his back to her, spreading a blanket on the
ground. It had a beautiful pattern, obviously Native
American, and it was woven in gorgeous hues of blue
and purple and rose. .

Would he pull her down onto that rainbow-colored
blanket and start kissing her? Or would he wait for her
to say, "I think I'll slip into something more comfortable," the way they did in the movies?

Mandy sighed. This was no movie, and she didn't have
a script. Furthermore, she was anxious about the rest of
the evening and was having dark, uncompromising
thoughts about her own sanity.

In fact, she was scared silly and probably looked it.
The last thing in the world she wanted to do was make

a fool of herself. Especially with Lucas Gray Wolf. Of all people, he was the one she most wanted to impress.

What would he think if she just didn't get out of her jeans?

What would he think if she did?

"Mandy? Is anything wrong?"

When the chips were down, be honest. That was her motto.

"I'm not sophisticated and worldly, Lucas." She raked her hand through her hair, certain that she now looked like a demonic porcupine. "I don't think I can do this."

Chapter Seven

Her simple honesty warmed Lucas's heart in ways he hadn't dreamed possible.

He was accustomed to another kind of woman entirely. Not that he was a playboy. Not by any stretch of the imagination. He simply adhered to the philosophy that man was not meant to be alone, at least not all the time. The occasional companion he sought was always as eager as he for the fleeting comforts of the flesh.

But here was something unexpected, a woman whose deeply ingrained morals waged a battle with her obvious desire. Her face was a study in longing and regret.

Lucas heard the faint rattling of rusty armor and realized with a start that it was his own. Something noble and chivalrous rose up in him as he mentally donned the little-used trappings of a gallant knight.

"Mandy, I'm not going to pretend I don't understand

what you mean. Both of us know why I invited you here, and I can't say I'm very proud of that.''

Her blush was the color of the sunset that streaked across the sky. With her warm cheeks and tousled red hair she looked like a painting by Titian.

''I'm sorry,'' she said, her voice as soft as the wind that stirred the trees and her eyes glinting with a hint of tears.

''Don't be. Don't you ever be sorry. I'm certainly not. You're the best company I've had since I left Arizona.''

''I suspect you're making that up. But thank you, anyway.''

Her smile was worth the trip. Her smile was worth the sleepless night he was certain to have.

''I'm not making up one bit of it, Lady. There's nothing I'd rather do right now than watch that spectacular sunset, and nobody I'd rather watch it with than you.''

He knelt at her feet and kissed her hands, loving the way she laughed, loving the way he felt, decent and carefree, unfettered by messy emotions such as guilt and regret, the kind of man he would want to take his sister to the movies. If he had a sister.

''You're a good man, Lucas Gray Wolf.''

''Shh. I don't want word to get around. It might ruin my reputation.''

He had her laughing, which was exactly what he intended. They walked to the river, arms hooked, hips and legs occasionally touching in a companionable and altogether satisfying way.

Who said sex was the greatest high? Lucas felt as if he owned the world.

When they came to the bluff overlooking the river, Lucas spread his blue jean jacket for Mandy, then sat beside her with his arm draped casually around her shoulders, holding her close enough to say *I'm here,* but not tight enough to be threatening.

"Are you ready for the best show in town, Lady?"

"You bet."

"Drumroll, please." Lucas picked up a couple of sticks and beat out the rhythm on the rock. Then, sweeping his arm toward the west, he said, "I give you the sun."

Startled by his announcement, a lone eagle flapped up and was soon swallowed by the brilliant streamers shooting across the sky. The sun was sinking over the river, scattering bits of gold across the water. Color shimmered around the waterbirds, so that they appeared to be dancing.

"I've never seen a more beautiful sunset," Mandy said.

Lucas liked to think he was the reason. "You should see them in Arizona. The sky is endless, and the color goes on forever."

He pictured how it would be, Mandy sitting astride one of the fine fillies from his stable, her hands resting lightly on the saddle horn, her reins within reach as the two of them watched the sun go down over the Verde River.

"It's so beautiful here, I don't want to go," she said.

"We don't have to. We'll stay atop this rock till hunger drives us away."

She laughed. "Or rain."

"I never let rain drive me inside. There's nothing I love better than turning my face up to a good rain shower."

"What about wild animals?"

"You have your very own Wolf to protect you. Don't you know that?"

"Hmm. I suppose I do."

She leaned against him, fitting her head into the crook of his shoulder as naturally as if she were born to be there. Lucas tightened his hold. He loved the feel of her, the fragrance of her, like sunshine and honeysuckle mingled together and blended with her skin and her hair.

I could get used to this, he thought.

The sky changed from sun-shot gold to a soft purple that dropped around them like a velvet curtain.

"All we need is music to make this perfect," she said, and Lucas started humming the first song that popped into his head.

"Is that from *Carousel*?" Mandy asked.

"Yes," he said, realizing with chagrin that it was, and that furthermore it was one of the most famous love songs ever written. What would Mandy think?

"It's beautiful. Sing the words, Lucas. Please."

She was soft and sweet, the night was warm and lovely. How could he refuse?

Lucas began to sing. Suddenly, a cloud of butterflies lifted from the wild flowers growing along the riverbank, and drifted upward on wings turned silvery in the light of a new moon floating over the river.

Mandy caught her breath. "Lucas, look. Did you ever see anything like it?"

"Never."

There was magic in the air and he didn't want to lose it.

"I planned this especially for you." Sweeping his arm wide, he said, "I gave you the sun and now I give you the moon, the river, the wind and the butterflies."

"And music. Don't forget the music." Sighing, she snuggled closer to him, her head tucked under his chin, her palm spread over his heart. "Keep singing." He would have chosen another, but she added, "The same song, please."

The wind sighed around them and the waves lapped softly against the shore. One of the butterflies separated from its companions and landed on Mandy's arm, where it sat fanning its wings. It didn't even fly away when Lucas began to sing the lyrics to "If I Loved You."

Lucas couldn't say precisely the moment she fell asleep, he just knew that she had. She lay against him loose and trusting, as innocent as a child. He shifted her so that he could see her face, and the butterfly took flight.

She was beautiful in her sleep, long eyelashes resting against silky cheeks, heart-shaped mouth slightly parted, damp curls feathered across her forehead. He'd never watched a woman sleeping. On the occasions he'd shared an intimacy with one, he'd turned away immediately afterward to lose himself in his own sleep.

Mandy looked vulnerable in her sleep, as fragile as a porcelain doll. He wondered about her ex-husband, wondered how a woman like Mandy had survived a man who could so callously—and foolishly—walk off with another woman.

What layers of courage lay hidden beneath that fair skin? What strength of character caused her to forge not only a tightly-knit family, but also a business, out of the shambles?

Surrounded by stars and cooled by the wind, Lucas stayed on the bluff overlooking the river until time and place ceased to exist. He was man, primeval, atavistic, protecting the woman cradled against his heart.

She stirred, smiling in her sleep at a dream that had pleased her. Lucas brushed her hair back from her forehead then leaned down and kissed her lips softly, tenderly.

"May the Great Creator always hold you in the palm of His hand, Mandy," he whispered.

Taking care not to wake her, Lucas carried her back to their campsite.

Chapter Eight

Startled out of sleep, Mandy tried to get her bearings. Fully dressed except for her boots, she lay on Lucas's multicolored blanket with another blanket tangled at her feet.

She always kicked off the covers. Chuck used to complain endlessly.

Of course, she wasn't with Chuck; she was with Lucas. He lay a few feet away from her, sleeping on the grass flat on his back with his blue jean jacket pillowing his head.

The last thing she remembered was being at the river listening to him sing. She must have fallen asleep, then he'd brought her back to camp and given her both blankets.

Tenderness welled up in Mandy and two fat tears rolled down her cheeks.

"What manner of man are you, Lucas Gray Wolf?" she whispered, but she already knew the answer.

He was a tough, danger-loving loner on the outside and a compassionate softy inside. He was a man who knew his way around a song as well as he knew his way around a motorbike. He called himself a wolf but acted like a perfect gentleman.

"I could love a man like you," she said softly. Her spontaneous confession startled her, and she squinted into the darkness to be certain Lucas was still sleeping. Then she looked behind her as if somebody might be hiding behind a tree listening.

Mandy Belinda couldn't afford to fall in love. She had children to care for, a business to run, a mother to look after, a living to make. She had responsibilities.

The weight of them bore her back to the blanket, and she lay there rigid. Then the plaintive call of an owl sounded in the distance. A soft summer breeze stirred the air and stars winked at her through the canopy of leaves.

She was in the middle of the woods, not in the heart of small-town Saltillo. She was unencumbered by children, work and worry. When she'd left home, her plan had been to seize the moment, to grab every bit of happiness she could. To cram so much pleasure into a few days that it would last her a lifetime.

Well, why not? Didn't she deserve it? And didn't he?

Moving quietly, Mandy shucked her clothes. Every single stitch. Then she riffled through her belongings till she found what she sought.

The package in her hand winked at her, and she winked back. Then she slipped off the cellophane and set to work.

Wouldn't Lucas be surprised?

Something brushed against Lucas. *Somebody.* In one

smooth motion he rolled over, taking the intruder with him. She stared back at him, wide-eyed.

"Mandy?"

"I wanted to surprise you."

"You succeeded."

"I'm sorry."

His full weight was on top of her. She was feeling boneless and fragile. And totally naked. She'd surprised him in more ways than one.

"I'm the one who's sorry. Did I hurt you?"

"No. I'm fine."

He lifted off her, and she lay against the grass, her skin gleaming with stars. They winked at him from every soft curve and luscious crevice of her body, tiny silver stick-on stars.

"You gave me the moon, the wind, the river, the butterflies," she said. "The least I can do is give you the stars."

Awestruck, he could only whisper her name.

"You don't think I'm awful?"

"I think you're incredible." He lifted her left hand and pressed a soft kiss in her palm. "This is the most wonderful gift anyone has ever given me."

With a deep, satisfied sigh, she stretched, arching her back in a way that heated his blood.

"I want you to touch the stars, Lucas." He already was. He'd started that about the time he'd realized she wasn't wearing any clothes.

"Why don't you start with Cassiopeia?" she whispered.

He traced the sparkling trail of silver that framed the soft mounds of her breasts, loving the way she responded, with sharp intakes of breath and tightening nipples. Lucas danced his fingertips around the dark areolas, then lowered his mouth over one of the diamond-hard tips.

Mandy became electrified, and the jolts shook Lucas clear down to his toes. He'd never experienced such sensations. Not with any other woman. Not ever. If anybody had told him such a thing was possible he'd have said they were crazy.

It was a miracle, plain and simple. Nothing less could explain why he was suddenly ten feet tall and owned the world.

He'd not only touched the stars, he'd touched the heavens.

Lucas swept her into his arms and carried her to the blanket where he spread her out like a sacred offering, a gift to the gods. His eyes were dark and piercing, his hair blown by the wind, his face so full of passion it almost hurt to look.

"I don't want the sticks and stones to hurt you," he said, and there was something in his voice so fiercely protective, so intensely possessive, that Mandy shivered.

"Are you cold?" he asked.

"A little." It was a bald-faced lie. She'd never been hotter in her life. Her blood was on fire, her skin, even the roots of her hair. Desire burned her from the tips of her toes to the top of her head.

"Don't worry. I'll cover you."

His chest gleaming in the moonlight, Lucas stripped off his pants. He was natural and unselfconscious about his own nudity, and so Mandy gave herself permission to stare. His was the most glorious male body she'd ever seen. Kneeling beside her, he looked like one of the magnificent bronzes done by Remington.

"You take my breath away," she said, quite simply,

then she did the most natural thing in the world—she touched him. Hesitantly at first, then with a sureness that shook all her long-held notions about herself. Overnight, she had turned into a bold, sensual woman.

She discovered the corded muscle and sinew of his arms, traced every inch of his chest, memorized the flat planes of his belly.

"See what you do to me," he whispered, his voice deepened by passion. "Touch me again, Mandy."

The Mandy who got up every morning at five-thirty and poured milk and cereal into stoneware bowls for three hungry children vanished. The wanton woman who took her place brazenly explored Lucas Gray Wolf, every enticing inch of him. Pleasure she'd never known swamped her as she explored his passion-gorged body with fingertips, then lips and tongue.

"Lady, your hands and mouth should be declared lethal weapons."

Cat-like, she purred and preened. If there had been a sunny windowsill, she'd have perched there basking in the glow of his praise. Still, there was some small part of her that disbelieved.

"It must be the stars," she said.

Bracketing her face with both hands, Lucas leaned so close his mouth almost touched hers. "It's *you,* Mandy. You're a sexy, exciting woman, with or without the stars."

His mouth closed over hers, and his kiss affirmed in a thousand ways everything he'd said. Mandy bloomed like a rose, opening herself to him petal by petal, soaking him up as if he were the moon, the sun, the rain.

"Speaking of stars…" He lowered his mouth over Cassiopeia once more. Mandy arched her back and cupped the sides of her breasts, offering herself up to him, a chalice to the gods.

Sensations rocked her, and her body quickened so that she could do nothing but writhe beneath him, her soft murmuring begging for more.

Panther-like, he crouched above her, his eyes gleaming as he took in all her constellations.

"What's this?" he whispered, his fingertips tracing a path of silver down her midsection.

"Orion."

His eyes gleamed. "The hunter? How perfect."

He grazed each twinkling orb with his tongue, and one by one the stars exploded, leaving their blazing trails across Mandy's hot skin. By the time he reached Orion's foot, she was almost incoherent with desire.

He pressed burning kisses into her triangle of dark curls, and when he parted her swollen secret core, his sharp intake of breath drove her wild.

"You've found..."

"No, let me guess. Venus, no doubt."

He slipped his fingers past the goddess of love, and the reply she'd formed died an instant and fiery death. There was magic in his hands. A force unlike any she'd ever known built in her, and when Lucas pressed his tongue to her hot core, she exploded. His lips continued their magic till Mandy was stretched taut as a piano wire, legs trembling, belly contracted. There was a tornado inside her, a hurricane, an earthquake.

"Please." Her voice was a hoarse whisper. "Please."

Lucas lifted his head to look at her. "Let yourself go, Mandy. Let it go."

Then his mouth closed over her once more, and she shattered into a million bright pieces. Suddenly, she was aware of the blanket under her back, the wind in the leaves, the moon riding the treetops, the stars falling from the sky.

Lucas smoothed back her damp hair and kissed her hot face and murmured to her in a language so sweet she thought she would cry. Then, one by one, he began to rediscover her stars, starting with the Milky Way wrapped round her throat.

By the time he got to Orion's belt she was a wild woman, begging with clutching hands and animal-like sounds to be released from her exquisite torture. With maddening tenderness, Lucas braced himself and slid toward Venus.

With arms and legs, Mandy imprisoned him, holding him tightly, savoring the feel of him inside her. She was a woman complete, a woman fulfilled.

"I don't want to ever let you go," she whispered, knowing all the while that she was marking herself as an unsophisticated woman. But what did she care? For the moment, all Mandy cared about was the marvelous oneness, the sense of being safe, being secure, being home.

"I won't let go," he murmured, then he began a slow, sweet rhythm that Mandy recognized. His body was singing a tune that had haunted her for years, a tune she'd been searching for without even knowing. A tune that could only be called love.

I've fallen in love, she thought, but for once she kept quiet. The truth would send him running, and Mandy wasn't prepared for that. Not yet.

If she played her cards right she had days left with this man. Long, lazy days and soft, steamy nights. And she intended to take advantage of every single moment.

Arching high against him, she said, "Make love to me, Lucas."

"You're so small. I don't want to hurt you."

"You won't."

"You're sure?"

"Positive. Love me, Lucas," she whispered fiercely. "Love me hard."

Unleashed, he was primitive, savage, thrusting with a power that drove her backward on the blanket. Mandy clutched fistfuls of blanket, anchoring herself, then opened the doors of her cage and turned loose a wild thing that took away the last remnant of reason.

"Incredible," he murmured.

Lifting her hips and lacing her legs around his waist, he drove into her until they were both panting. Then he rolled onto his back, taking her with him. Sweat rolled down her cheeks and between her breasts and thighs, and they clung to each other, slick and steamy, while loosened stars fell around them.

"How're you doing, Lady?" he whispered.

"Great...stupendous...glorious." She spoke between short bursts of breath.

"Then love me." His hips took up an erotic rhythm. "Love me till the dawn."

Did he say love, or was she dreaming? Mandy didn't have time to ponder the question, for her body was already rising to the challenge.

Closing her eyes, she rocked a gentle rhythm while the moon tracked across the sky. The fierceness of passion began to grow in them, escalating to gale proportions.

"Yes," Lucas whispered. "Yes."

Then catching her hands, Lucas held her steady while they entered the eye of the storm. Mandy thought she would die of love.

When the first faint fingers of dawn painted the sky, Lucas cried out and spilled his seed.

She *was* dying...and already in heaven.

Chapter Nine

Lucas always woke up hungry. He had been that way as long as he could remember. As soon as the sun came up, he'd be out of bed looking for the nearest food, preferably a logger's breakfast of bacon and eggs and hash browns served with biscuits big as wagon wheels.

Then why was he sitting on the blanket staring at Mandy sleeping like a man besotted? How could one night in her arms change lifelong patterns? How could one lovemaking session turn him into a man who thrilled at the way her eyelashes lay across her cheeks, at the way her skin was still flushed where he'd touched her?

Where he wanted to touch her again. Now.

Desire lay coiled inside him, so intense it was almost painful. Fool that he was, Lucas stared down at her, hoping a leaf would drop on her cheek and wake her up, hoping a squirrel would start a fight with a mockingbird, hoping an owl would call her name. Anything. Anything to get Mandy to open her eyes and want him. Want him as much as he wanted her.

"Lucas?" She opened her eyes, then smiled at him, still slightly groggy with sleep.

Could thoughts become so powerful they provoked action? "Hello, Lady," he murmured, then bent down to kiss her.

"Come here, you." She laced her arms around his neck, and that was all the invitation he needed. Parting her thighs with one leg, he slid home.

Mandy had packed almond cream cheese croissants for breakfast. Homemade from her bakery.

"I never tasted anything so delicious in my life," Lucas told her. Then quickly amended, "With a notable exception or two."

She blushed, or was that still the flush of love on her skin? She hoped so. She hoped he kept her skin pink with the glow. She hoped he made love to her so many times that she'd glow for weeks after she returned to Saltillo.

Days. Months.

"Best breakfast I ever had," he said.

Mandy squinted at the sun, high in the sky. "Or is it lunch?"

Lucas grinned. "I don't care, do you?"

"No. I didn't bring my watch."

"Good. I don't even wear one."

Hope leaped in her heart. They would forget time. Maybe time would even stand still and a thousand days with Lucas in the woods would seem as only a day in Saltillo.

But even a thousand days would not be enough. Deep

in her heart, Mandy knew that nothing less than a lifetime and beyond would be enough with her magnificent Sioux.

"What was that beautiful language you spoke last night?" she said.

"The language of my ancestors."

"What were you saying?"

"It was an ancient Sioux chant."

"Tell me the words."

Lucas looked into the distance as if he were seeking help from an unknown source. "It was spontaneous," he said.

"I want to know the words." She wanted to know and remember every word he spoke. She wanted to observe every small detail of their time together. "Please, Lucas."

"I can never refuse you anything."

Mandy had a hard time not making more of his statement than he meant. *Careful,* she told herself. If she took everything he said to heart, she would be setting herself up for heartbreak.

But hadn't she done that already? The minute she'd set out to the woods with him, knowing the outcome, she'd set a rocky course for herself.

Don't even think about trying to change things, she told herself. *Seize the moment.*

"Close your eyes," he said. "Pretend there's a full moon. Ready?"

"Ready."

"'Mother Earth opens herself, spreads herself wide for Father Sky. His snow falls lightly upon her brow. His rains are gentle upon her breasts. And when he turns his flood upon her, she receives him, and becomes fertile.'"

"That's so beautiful I could cry."

"You already are." Lucas caught her tears on his fingertips, then pressed them to his lips where he licked the dampness away.

Unconsciously, Mandy leaned forward, and he offered his fingers to her. She took them deep in her mouth, savoring their texture, curling her tongue around their shape.

Lucas groaned. "What are you doing to me, Lady?"

"Whatever you want," she whispered.

He slid her shirt from her shoulders, then, never taking his eyes from hers, he began to knead her breasts. Her response was instant. Lucas massaged the taut tips until she cried out, "More. I want more."

"I love it when you say that."

Gently he peeled away the rest of her clothes, then his own.

"Kneel facing me, Mandy."

She didn't ask why. Only a fool would question the gift of paradise.

"You gave me the constellations, and now I give you mine. Hold my hands, Mandy. That's it. Together we form the circle of the sky spirits or the constellation Corona Borealis. Within this circle, we will find our deepest selves."

Mandy's blood began to heat up. It took so little with this man, a single touch, the sound of his voice. But this was how she loved him best, naked and untamed, immersed in the rituals of his ancestors.

His eyes raked over her, hot as burning coals, then he cupped her breasts, lifting them as if they were an offering.

"You are the earth mother from which springs all life. Flower buds lie within you, the souls of trees, the hearts of meadowlands longing to be green."

His thumb moved in erotic circles around her nipples,

and a involuntary spasm shook her from head to toe. Only Lucas could do that to her. Only her magnificent Gray Wolf.

"Within your fertile valley lie the seeds of mankind waiting for the power of the sun." When he dipped his fingers into her swollen sex, he became fully aroused. Moving with languid rhythm, his fingers brought her to the edge of climax.

"You are earth and I am sun. Claim the heat, Mandy, claim the power."

His skin gleamed with sweat, every inch of it like burnished copper, and Mandy knew he spoke the truth. He *was* the sun and she was in his orbit.

"Dance, Mandy," he whispered. "Dance with the sun."

Need overwhelmed her, made her knees weak. She didn't know how much longer she could stay upright. Lucas reached out and steadied her. Was he reading her mind?

"Lucas…" She couldn't go on, couldn't put words to her thoughts. Passion was a whirlpool and she was drowning.

"Your wish is my command, sweet Lady," he whispered, then leaned forward and with his other hand traced an erotic line from her throat to her flat belly.

He used his mouth next, and Mandy became undone. Heavy with desire, she went limp all over. Lucas scooped her up and carried her to the blanket. She barely saw its colors, barely felt its downy texture. Lucas controlled her world.

"Lucas, I'm…" *What? Too limp to move? Too far gone to think? Dying with love?* Her mind had vanished. There was nothing left of her except her will and her heart, and both she gave to Lucas.

"Shh, don't try to talk. Just follow me."

With soft murmurings and gentle hands he guided her onto all fours. Then kneeling behind her and supporting her belly with his hands, he gave her paradise.

Pinwheels of color spun before her eyes, trees and vines and bushes danced, the world turned upside down. Mandy had never felt such freedom, such eroticism, such joy. Filled with Lucas, filled with abandon, she took up his wild rhythm, her hoarse pleasure cries echoing through the forest.

Time no longer existed. Daylight and darkness didn't matter. There was nothing except the two of them and the erotic world they'd created.

Sweat dripped onto the blanket, his mingled with hers. Small details imprinted into Mandy's mind—the feel of the hard earth underneath her knees, the crumpled blanket in her fists, the feel of satin-sheathed steel in her body.

The power of Lucas amazed her, overwhelmed her, thrilled her. Time and again he brought her to screaming climax, and time and again he pulled himself back from the edge. Her arms trembled, her whole body shook with passion.

And when she thought there was nothing else left in her, Lucas proved her wrong.

"Now, Mandy, now," he shouted, and they erupted together.

Then Lucas guided her gently downward where they lay spooned on the blanket. Sleepy and sated, she closed her eyes, and her last thought before she drifted into sleep was *How can I bear for him to leave me?*

Chapter Ten

When they woke up, they frolicked in the river like children. Then Lucas made a spear and caught their dinner.

"In the ancient way," he said proudly. "Once a Sioux, always a Sioux."

They grilled his catch over the open fire, then leaned into each other and listened to the night music of God's creatures.

"Shall we dance, Mandy?"

She laughed softly, her color deepened. "Again?" she whispered, and it was his turn to laugh.

He kissed the tip of her nose. "Tired of me already?"

"Absolutely not. In fact, I can't get enough of you."

"Hmm, a woman after my own heart, but do you mind if we make our dance the old-fashioned kind this time?"

"Oh, I love dancing. I haven't danced since goodness knows when. But where's the music, Lucas?"

He began to hum. "Do you know that song, Mandy?"
"No."

"'Quiet Nights of Quiet Stars,' because you gave me
the stars."

Mandy was a natural dancer, and they fell into perfect
rhythm while the stars came out one by one. Cocooned
under the brilliant night sky, Lucas dreamed he might
stay in the woods forever, with Mandy in his arms.

But another night was upon them, another day approached. No matter how he willed it, time didn't stand
still. Back in Arizona, Paradise Ranch waited for him,
and the road home was long.

One more day with Mandy. That's all he would allow
himself.

She leaned her head against his shoulder, and he began
to sing the words to the song. Venus seemed caught in
Mandy's bright hair, and he knew that he would never
look at another star without thinking of her.

His song ended, and they curled into each other heart
to heart and drifted, sleeping and dreaming, until desire
sent them spiraling once more to the stars.

Mandy lay quietly on the blanket watching Lucas
sleep. It was almost too rich to bear, waking up beside
Lucas instead of in her lonely bed. Comfort and strength
lay beside her, passion and protection, love and laughter—all the things a woman cherished, all the things she
wanted to keep forever.

But the fates had other plans for Mandy. She sighed.
Why had they sent her the one man she could never have,
and then on top of that, arranged for her to fall in love
with him?

He opened his eyes and lay perfectly still. His solemn
regard was unnerving. Premonition made Mandy shiver.

Lucas was leaving.

"Cold?" He reached for her.

"Yes," she said, lying.

"We'll have to do something about that," he said, and then he did.

Afterward, he took maps from his backpack. "Have you ever been caving, Mandy?"

She shivered, thinking of Rusty. "No, and I'm not sure I want to."

"They are really quite beautiful. There are about seven thousand in this area, one I'd especially like to see before we leave. It's called Rainbow Cave."

There, he'd said it. Before we leave.

Her heart dropped to her knees. *Play it cool,* she told herself. *You knew this was coming.*

"All I can picture is that dark hole that swallowed Rusty," she said.

"Not all of them are like that. You have to rappel down some of them, but others have entrances that you walk or crawl into."

"Still, all that blackness at the bottom. And what about bats?"

"Come here, you." Lucas pulled Mandy close and hugged her. "We're not going to do a single thing that you don't want to do." He tossed the map aside. "Forget about caves and caving."

Mandy loved nothing better than hugging. Almost nothing, she amended, thinking of the two of them tangled together on the blanket. She was perfectly content to stay cuddled up with Lucas for the rest of the morning, the rest of the trip, the rest of her lifetime.

But Lucas was not a domestic animal. She'd known it the moment she laid eyes on him. He craved adventure and probably always would. He traveled the open road on a GoldWing and refused even to live in a house.

Before we leave. His words echoed in her mind. She wanted every moment to be perfect for him. When he left, she wanted him to have nothing except beautiful memories.

"About that cave..." she said after a bit. "If we go, do you have everything we need?"

"Yes. Are you sure you want to?"

"Positive." She smiled at him. "I trust you, Lucas."

"I promise you won't regret this."

The cave, located a few miles from their campsite, was an easy ride on Lucas's GoldWing. On the highest ridge along the river, its entrance almost hidden by under-growth, Rainbow Cave was one of the largest in the area, with five entrances.

"Scared, Mandy?"

"A little. But I'm not backing out."

"This one has been well-explored. And it's a favorite with children." He squeezed her hand. "Are you ready?"

She took a deep breath. "They say when you fall off a horse, it's best to climb back on. Although I wasn't the one who fell off, figuratively speaking, I think I need to get back on." She raked her hand through her hair. "I'm sorry. I always chatter when I'm nervous."

"You can still change your mind."

"No. If there's one thing I have, it's courage."

"I'll go first and check things out. You follow close behind. Keep one hand on my foot, if you like."

On all fours, Mandy crawled into the opening. It wasn't as bad as she'd imagined until the entrance was out of sight. It was the most complete blackness Mandy had ever seen.

More than that, she heard scurryings and rustlings in the darkness.

Mandy panicked. "Lucas?"

"We're almost there. Hang on, Mandy, except not so tightly."

Mandy had had his foot in a death grip. She'd been hanging on the whole time, she realized. She had Lucas. What was there to worry about?

They burst suddenly out of the tunnel and into a vaulted cavern that echoed with the sounds of their voices. Water dripped down limestone walls, and a small underground pool lay just to their right.

Lucas shone the beam of his flashlight around, and Mandy caught her breath. Formations of gypsum, curly as bacon fried in Grandma Bailey's iron skillet, dripped from the ceiling.

"It's beautiful," she said.

"Wait till you see what's in store." Lucas caught her hand. "The floor is slick in places. Watch your step."

Winding their way around enormous rock formations, they left the entry chamber and entered a dark passageway barely wide enough for them to pass. Her only compensation was that she had Lucas's hand to hang onto.

"Where are we going?" she said.

"One of the most beautiful spots in the world. It's not far, if I read the map right."

Mandy's heart plummeted to her knees. What if he hadn't? What if they had to spend the next few hours wandering around in these cramped spaces? She'd die of claustrophobia.

She was glad it was too dark for Lucas to see her face. He'd think she was a complete wimp. His opinion mattered to Mandy so much that she scared herself. One of the reasons she'd been able to forge her little family back together after Chuck left was that she'd done whatever was necessary despite what anybody else said. Even her mother.

"You ought to get a nice job somewhere instead of struggling to start a business," Evelyn had said. "Who's going to buy cakes and pies in this town? Everybody bakes their own."

Mandy had proved her mother wrong.

And now, here she was working herself into a tizzy over a man who had already declared his intention of leaving. Was that the reason women stayed in impossible marriages, impossible work conditions and impossible relationships? They were afraid of what people would think?

She wasn't about to turn into one of those women. She couldn't afford to. She had three children to raise. Alone.

Face it, she told herself. Their idyll in the woods was over, and Lucas was going to ride off on his GoldWing bike and never look back. And then what would Mandy do?

The same as always. She would survive. But if that were going to happen, she'd better take control, starting right now.

The first thing she did was let go of Lucas's hand. After all, he was shining a flashlight along the path. She had eyes, didn't she? She could see.

"Mandy? Is everything okay?"

"Great." That was a bald-faced lie. From the minute he'd mentioned leaving, she'd been anything except great.

"I think it's just up ahead," he said. "The surprise."

The biggest surprise to Mandy was that she'd managed, so far, to forget that she was the sole support of three children. Chuck's child-support payments had been sporadic at best, then had finally petered out altogether.

He'd become a self-involved person seeking only his own pleasure, and now, so had Mandy. That was how powerful Lucas's effect on her was.

It was time for a reality check. She was going to build an armor around her heart.

The narrow passageway ended abruptly, and they popped into a cavern so enormous it looked like a cathedral. A lake of clearest crystal lay on its floor, and what was more, a small opening in the ceiling let in a small beam of natural light. Gypsum hung like lace curtains.

In the dying light of the sun, the gypsum formations became prisms. Rainbows danced over the walls and across the water.

"Do you like it, Mandy?" Lucas said, softly.

"Like it? I *love* it."

"I'm glad. It's my gift to you." He reached for her hand, and her hastily erected armor cracked, then tumbled. "I wanted to give you a rainbow."

Face it. She was never going to be the kind of woman who could skim over the surface of a situation and leave her heart and her emotions behind. She was always going to be wide open to joy—and wide open to heartbreak.

"Tears?" His voice was as tender as his hands.

"Beauty sometimes moves me to tears." She wasn't telling a lie, but she wasn't telling the whole truth, either.

He didn't challenge her. Instead he wiped her face dry with his fingertips, then pulled her close and kissed the tip of her nose.

What was she going to do when she no longer had this sort of warmth within her reach? She tried to ease out of his arms, but he had other plans.

Rocks formed natural seating, and Lucas pulled her down beside him.

"Comfortable?" he said.

"Yes."

"Good. Now sit very still." He cupped her face and turned it slightly toward the cave's small opening. Red and purple and blue and gold streaked across her hands and arms. She was in the middle of the rainbow.

"I want to remember you this way, Mandy." He touched her face, her hair. "Gold at the end of the rainbow."

I will not cry, she told herself.

"You're leaving, then?"

"Today. I have to get back to the ranch."

She nodded. "I understand."

They looked at each other, then their gazes slid away. They tracked the path of the rainbow, the trickle of water on the limestone walls, the pattern of gypsum hanging from the ceilings. Every detail of the cave claimed their undivided attention.

"Lucas," Mandy said touching his cheek, "look at me."

His face was a careful mask, and the humor that always lit his eyes had vanished. Lucas Gray Wolf had already gone and left her in the company of a stranger.

"I want you to know that this has been the best time of my life," she said. "When we leave here I will have no regrets. Not a single one."

"You're sure about that, Lady?"

"Absolutely."

Lucas was back: he'd used his pet name for her. She leaned against him, her head on his shoulder. He drew her closer, then rested his chin on her hair.

They stayed that way while the sun-kissed crystals

painted colors on their skin. As far as Mandy was concerned, it was a fairy-tale ending for a fairy-tale romance.

The only things missing were declarations of undying love and promises of happily ever after. *How can I let him leave without telling him that I love him?*

Telling would spoil everything. She knew that. He would leave anyway, leave with a load of guilt knowing he'd broken her heart. And yet, she had to let him know that he was more than a passing fancy for her, that the last few days had been more than a careless fling.

A bright swatch of deep rose danced off the crystals, and Mandy caught it in the palm of her hand. Then she cupped Lucas's face, imagining she carried the color with her.

"It's important that I tell you something, Lucas," she whispered, and when he fixed her with a solemn gaze, his eyes had taken on that deep-turquoise color she'd seen as she lay on the blanket with Lucas poised above her.

"I'm listening."

"I want you to know that no man has ever given me a rainbow. No man except you."

"Thank you."

His response wasn't much, but it was enough that his eyes had turned the color of love.

Chapter Eleven

Lucas had known that riding away from Mandy wouldn't be easy. What he hadn't expected was the overwhelming sense of loss.

She had stood under the streetlight in front of her bakery, waving and smiling bravely while he gunned the bike and felt as if he'd severed an arm or a leg. Or a heart.

"I'll take you to your house," he'd told her on the ride back to Saltillo, but she'd said, "No, it's better this way."

Her car was parked behind the bakery. She would drive home alone, just the way she'd come.

That's what they'd decided.

Then why did Lucas feel like a deserter? Why did he feel as if he were abandoning not only Mandy, but the children, too?

The radio was playing the theme song from "Maverick,'' which struck Lucas as appropriate. He was a maverick, wasn't he? A man who never traveled with more than he could fit into his knapsack? Then why, all of a sudden, did he feel so lonely?

He was approaching the outskirts of Saltillo. Even if he looked back, he probably couldn't see Mandy. And even if he could, she probably wasn't still there.

Lucas looked back. It was a mistake. There she was, her blouse a tiny spot of bright pink, still standing in front of her bakery. Lucky Mandy's.

He figured her luck had run out the day she met him. Furious without knowing why, Lucas revved his bike up to just below the speed of light.

''Don't say a word, Mother.''

Evelyn was sitting in a wing chair in the living room, dressed in her nightgown, staring at the TV. She'd recognized the sound of Mandy's car, then had come downstairs to wait. Mandy knew this without even asking. It was her mother's way.

Evelyn sniffed, pretending deep offense. That, too, was a sham. ''I didn't say a thing. Did I say a word?''

''No, but that's why you came down here. It's way past your bedtime.''

''I came down to watch television.''

''Then you'd better turn up the volume.'' The actors moved across the screen like stars in a silent movie.

Evelyn pursed her lips, then turned up the sound. Relieved, Mandy headed upstairs. She'd almost gained the stairs when Evelyn called out to her.

''I just want to know one thing. Did he propose?''

The sound Mandy made was a heart breaking in two. She squeezed back the tears that threatened to spill, then tried to learn how to breathe again.

"No, Mother," she said, "he didn't propose. And I didn't expect him to."

She hurried up the stairs before her mother could say anything else. Everything looked the same, the same pictures on the walls, the same rugs on the floor, the same curtains at the window. The same lonely bed.

Then why did she feel like a stranger in her own home? She didn't feel like Mandy Sullivan Belinda at all, but some other woman. A woman who knew passion. A woman who knew the feel of the moon on her naked skin. A woman who knew intimate secrets that would make most people blush.

A woman who knew love.

"I will not cry," she whispered, then started unpacking her knapsack. Cellophane rustled. The empty wrapper for the stars.

"No, I won't think about that."

Mandy put her hands over her face, and drew a deep breath. When she felt alive again, she tossed the knapsack into the corner of her closet. She couldn't deal with the memories right now. She would unpack tomorrow. Or maybe next week. Or maybe never.

She might simply throw the whole thing into the garbage can. Everything she'd worn reminded her in some way of Lucas, of love, of paradise.

Her legs were unsteady as she walked to the window. There was a full moon out tonight. Was Lucas still riding, or had he stopped somewhere along the way and spread his bedroll under the stars?

Mandy stripped in the dark. She couldn't bear to see herself, couldn't bear to see the skin that Lucas had touched, the pinkened patches where his beard had rubbed, the flush that still lay across her belly.

They had meant to do nothing more than sit in the

cave and watch the rainbow. But passion had claimed them quickly, as always.

Stripped of her clothes, hard limestone at her back, a rainbow across her thighs and Lucas across her heart, Mandy had lost all reason. Both of them had.

The possibility of being caught, of someone entering the cave and finding them, had added to the excitement. Still, their lovemaking had been unhurried.

Taking a piece of limestone, Lucas had marked their naked bodies with the ancient symbols of his Sioux ancestors.

"With these symbols I infuse us with the spirits of nature's creatures, the ones that swim in the deep, the winged ones, and the four-footed ones." The slash marks across his chest looked like claws. "I am Wolf," he said.

"And what am I?"

He circled her nipples with the makeshift chalk, then fanned the lines toward her ribs.

"You are a bird, my Lady bird who flies among the stars."

His eyes as deep as the pool at the bottom of the cave, he leaned over and brushed his lips across her breasts.

"You are my Lady," he whispered, then took up a rhythm that drove her wild.

Now and forever, she thought, and she told him the only way she could: she gave herself completely to Lucas Gray Wolf, heart, body and soul.

Swamped by memories, Mandy leaned her face against the cool windowpane. Moonlight fell across her skin, and there on her breasts was the mark of the Sioux.

Lucas had branded her, and she was his.

Chapter Twelve

It was three weeks before Lucas could bear to face the contents of his knapsack. Too many reminders.

Finally, he could put it off no longer. If he didn't unpack, his jeans would grow mold. There was only one way to do the job and that was quickly. He jerked his clothes out and tossed them into the washing machine, then grabbed the books Mandy's mother had given him and headed toward the kitchen.

He heard them before he saw them, Thunderhorse and Angel, laughing at some private joke.

"I can't do this," Lucas muttered.

He didn't want to face all that wedded bliss. He didn't want to see how his best friend had overcome a tragic past to forge a beautiful future. He had much rather cling to his illusions. He had much rather tell himself that there was no such thing as a happy ending.

At least for some folks. Certainly, for him.

"Lucas. Is that you out there muttering to yourself?" Thunderhorse stuck his head around the door frame and grinned. "Get your butt in here. You're not interrupting anything."

"With the two of you, I never know." Lucas plopped onto a bar stool. "Good morning, Angel. You look radiant, as always."

"More radiant than usual, I hope."

She was teasing him. There wasn't a vain bone in her body, and besides, her grin was decidedly impish.

"You might say that." Lucas nabbed a raisin bran muffin from the plate. "These are good. Did you make them?"

"Me? The last time I tried to cook I nearly burned the kitchen down." Quick contrition colored her face. "I'm sorry, Lucas."

"No problem. The fires happened a long time ago." Steve was prowling around the kitchen like a big mountain cat, alternately grinning and looking pleased with himself. "What's got into you?" Lucas asked him.

Still grinning, he put his arms around his wife and gave her a kiss that left her flushed. "Do you want to tell him, Angel, or shall I?"

"Go ahead, darling. You've been bursting at the seams since last night."

"We're pregnant," Steve said. "I wanted you to be the first to know."

Lucas felt like a cad. His best friend had just shared some of the most important news a man could have, and Lucas sat on the stool like a toad, eaten up with envy and regret.

"Aren't you going to say something?" Steve prodded.

"I guess you rendered me speechless." He got up to

shake Steve's hand. "Congratulations. It couldn't happen to a better man."

"He's going to be a wonderful father." The look Angel gave her husband was filled with love and pride. As far as Lucas could tell, there was not a trace of anxiety on her face. Or on Steve's.

Lucas was glad. Considering what Steve had gone through after the tragic death of his daughter, Sunny, this turn of events was nothing short of a miracle.

A vision of Mandy standing beside the river barefoot and laughing came to Lucas's mind. *Only one miracle per household,* he reminded himself. And he was certainly a part of Steve Thunderhorse's household, even if he did sleep under the stars more than he slept under the roof.

"When is the big event?" Lucas asked.

"Sometime around Christmas. It's perfect. Last Christmas I captured one Angel, and this Christmas I'll have another one."

Happiness should be doled out in small doses for some men, and Lucas counted himself among them. He had to get out of the kitchen before he smothered.

He'd started to leave when the books on the bar caught his eye.

"I almost forgot. Will you sign these, Angel?"

"Of course." She got her pen from the kitchen desk. "Who are they for?"

"Evelyn Sullivan."

Steve lifted an eyebrow. "Is there something you're not telling us, Lucas?" Lucas nabbed his hat off the hat rack and stonewalled, but Steve wouldn't be put off. "You haven't said anything about your trip. How was it?"

"Great." That was the understatement of the year, but

Lucas wasn't about to go into any explanations or even self-examinations as to why that should be so.

"Would this Miss Sullivan have anything to do with your good time?"

"Give it a rest, Steve. She's seventy if she's a day. Ever since you got married you've been hot on my trail to follow suit." He rammed his hat on his head. "I'm out of here."

"Darling, you shouldn't be so hard on him," Angel said, as Lucas stalked toward the back door. "Lucas, wait. You forgot the books."

"Thanks, Angel." The first thing he was going to do was put them in the mail and then he'd be through with all of them—with Evelyn and her ideas of romance, with Rusty who desperately wanted a daddy, with Jill whose soft cheeks reminded him of duck's down, with Betsy who regarded him as nothing less than an oracle, with Mandy...especially with Mandy.

He couldn't bear to think of the things she brought to mind. Back in the bunkhouse, he hastily scrawled out the address, then climbed on his GoldWing and roared off to the post office. The sooner he got rid of the last reminder of Mandy, the sooner he would forget her.

Mississippi had the hottest August on record. Mandy guessed it was the heat that kept the women of Saltillo out of their kitchens and sent them scurrying to Lucky Mandy's for their baked goods. Whatever the reason, she wasn't about to look a gift horse in the mouth.

Business boomed. She was on her feet all day and sometimes into the night filling orders. For the first time she could remember, the smell of sugar and cinnamon made her sick.

"I've got to take a break, Josie," she told her assistant. "Do you mind watching the front?"

"Of course not. You've been working too hard, Mandy. Look at those feet of yours."

Mandy didn't have to look. They felt like stuffed sausages. Three or four times a day, she found herself bending over to loosen her shoelaces.

Her office was tiny, nothing more than a walk-in closet, really, but it served Mandy's purposes. All she needed was enough space for a file cabinet, a small desk and a chair. Now, she wished for a recliner instead of the office chair that did nothing but swivel.

She sank into the chair and loosened her shoelaces, then on second thought, her waistband, too. Everything she had was getting too tight.

Grief sometimes did that to women. She'd known women who gained as much as fifty pounds because somebody broke their heart.

The smells of sugar and cinnamon wafted from the kitchen, overpowering her. She rested her head on the desk, then jumped up and raced to the bathroom.

Josie stuck her head through the door. "Are you all right in here?"

Mandy wiped her face with a damp cloth. "I'm fine. Just queasy, that's all."

"Why don't you go on home, get a little rest. Myrtle and I can handle things just fine."

Ordinarily, Mandy wouldn't have dreamed of such a thing, running out on her employees when there was so much work to be done. But today wasn't turning out to be an ordinary day, and so, for once, she didn't argue with Josie. Instead she said, "Thanks," then grabbed her purse and headed for the door.

Josie followed her, clucking over her like a mother

hen. Widowed for years, Josie still considered herself a married woman. "My only regret is that Lem and I didn't have children," she was fond of saying, as if she and Lem had been married sixteen years instead of sixteen days. "He never saw that train a-coming," was the way Josie told the story of his death. "I just wish I'd a-been in there with him."

Now she patted Mandy on the back. "A good rest and you'll be good as new in the morning."

She wasn't going to be good as new tomorrow nor the day after, either. The suspicion Mandy had had in the bathroom became a full-blown fact as she sat in the car with her head on the steering wheel counting backward. It had been eight weeks since she was with Lucas, ten since her last period.

Mandy didn't have to go to the drugstore for an early testing kit to know what that meant: she was pregnant. It wasn't sugar and cinnamon that was making her sick. It wasn't stress that caused her to be late. It was the child she carried in her womb. Lucas's baby.

Her reaction was part joy, part terror. Now she would always have a part of Lucas Gray Wolf with her, but could she raise the child alone?

Mandy jerked herself upright and gripped the wheel, chin held high. "I not only *can,* I *will.*" With that declaration, she hurried off to the drugstore, just to make sure.

She waited until after the children were in bed before she told her mother. "I'm pregnant," she said.

"You're what? The saints preserve us. We're doomed." Evelyn pressed her hand over her heart and sank into her chair. Her act was so convincing she might have invented the art of swooning. She fooled everybody except her daughter.

"Good grief, Mother, we're not doomed. We're going to have another mouth to feed, that's all. You love children as much as I do. Now sit up and help me plan for this baby."

Evelyn sat up straight and fluffed her hair. "I suppose it belongs to Lucas Gray Wolf."

"It definitely does. I haven't been with anybody else since Chuck left."

"You always could get pregnant at the drop of a hat."

"That's water under the bridge now, Mother. By next month I'll be as big as the Goodyear blimp. We have to decide how we're going to handle this."

What she'd said was true. There were women who could still wear their regular clothes at three months, and even at five if they wore their shirts on the outside. But not Mandy. She always carried her unborn babies proudly out front. When she went somewhere, they entered the room first like drum majorettes, waving flags and leading a brass band.

"I know how I'm going to handle it," Evelyn said, purse-lipped. "I'm going to call Lucas and tell him to get his fanny back to Mississippi and make an honest woman of you."

"Don't you dare! I don't want Lucas to know."

"Of course he has to know. He's the father. He has responsibilities."

"Chuck married me because of the same responsibilities, remember? And look how that turned out. I'm *never* going to hog-tie another man to my side with guilt."

"Lucas is not Chuck."

"No, he's not Chuck, but he's also not the marrying

kind, Mother. I knew that from the start. I took my chances, and now I'll face the consequences. Alone.''

"What are folks in town going to say?"

"I don't give a fig what they say, as long as they leave my children out of it. It's nobody's business what I do with my life."

"We could say you got married in Reno, then turned around three days later and got a divorce when you re- alized you'd made a mistake."

Mandy made a face, and Evelyn took off her glasses and began to polish the lenses.

"I still think you owe it to Lucas to let him know about this."

"Mother, Lucas values his freedom above all things. If I told him, he would surely do the right thing because he's that kind of man. And then he'd be miserable the rest of his life. I won't do that to him."

She knelt in front of her mother's chair and took her hand. "Promise you won't say anything to him."

Evelyn held her glasses up to the lamplight and con- sidered them.

"Mother, promise!"

Evelyn sighed. "All right. I promise."

"Thank you, Mother. You're a brick. You always have been."

"I do hope it's a boy. I rather fancy having a grandson who looks like Lucas Gray Wolf. He's about the hand- somest man I've ever laid eyes on. Except your father, of course."

Later, Mandy lay in bed with her palms pressed softly against her abdomen, humming to herself and dreaming.

She loved being pregnant. She always had. In spite of the occasional nausea and swelling, she always felt great. When she'd been pregnant with Jill she'd told Chuck she had enough energy to slipcover Texas if she had about eighty thousand yards of fabric.

He'd never shared her joy. To her ex-husband, her pregnancies were nothing but a huge inconvenience.

What would Lucas say if he knew? Would he thrill at the idea of having a small person who was flesh of his flesh? Would he rub her stomach with cocoa butter and press his face close to her big belly and sing to his unborn child? Would he be proud that his name would go on?

Mandy's glow faded. What would she call this child? Not Belinda. She couldn't bear the thought of Lucas's baby bearing Chuck's name.

A star winked at her through the window. Lucas had kissed her until all the stars she'd stuck on her skin came loose and fell to the ground, then they'd made love on a blanket of stars.

"You were conceived among the stars, little one," she whispered. "You were conceived in love, and you will always be loved."

Nothing else mattered. Not what she would call her child, not what people would say, not what Lucas would do if he found out.

Mandy rubbed the little mound of her belly, then cupped her breasts. Already they felt fuller. Soon her baby would suckle where Lucas had. And every time she looked down at him, she would see her beloved.

"I hope it's a boy, too, Mother," she whispered. "And I hope he looks just like his father."

Chapter Thirteen

September and October brought the worst thunderstorms Arizona had ever seen, and with them, flash flooding. Water rushed down the draws and roared across Paradise Ranch, threatening the horses. As far as Lucas was concerned, the only good thing about the floods were that they kept his mind off Mandy.

Since he'd left Mississippi, he'd thought of her day and night. It was enough to drive a man crazy.

In a way, the floods were his salvation. He and Steve worked from dawn till way after dark moving their herds of horses to higher ground, rescuing stragglers, fighting the elements.

It rained so much that the old bunkhouse where Lucas always slept, which hadn't been renovated in years, sprang a leak in the roof. Water stood knee-deep on the floor, forcing Lucas to move his bedroll to the main house.

That's where his trouble started all over again. Seeing Steve and Angel together made him think of Mandy—not only think of her but think of how it might have been between them if he were different.

Lucas would stand in the shadows watching them kiss, not to spy, but because he'd been headed into the room anyway and didn't want to intrude. Didn't they deserve a chance to be together? Steve's hearing was acute, and even Sioux stealth wouldn't get Lucas out of sight before his friend saw him. And there would go romance, right out the window.

Lucas spent many an evening in dark corners waiting for a marital kiss to heat up to the point that he could safely leave without Steve noticing him. Then, flopped on the bed in his room, trapped by the storm outside and the romance inside, Lucas would relive every moment he'd spent with Mandy. By mid-October, he was a wreck.

"You look like hell," Steve said to him at breakfast. "Is sleeping in a house that bad for you?"

"Yes, it's that bad."

"Remember what you told me when I went so crazy the day Angel got lost? You said it was time for me to put the past behind."

"That's what you're telling me, huh?"

"Something like that. I'm also telling you to go after this woman you've been mooning over for months."

"How did you know?"

Steve threw back his head and roared with laughter. "I got bit by the same bug. I recognize the symptoms."

Angel came into the kitchen, her hands cupped lovingly around her heavy womb. "Who are you calling a bug?" She kissed her husband soundly on the mouth, then stood beside him ruffling his hair.

Steve pulled her into his lap, grunting with fake effort. "You're getting to be a load, there, bug."

Angel made a face at him, then kissed him again. Thoroughly.

Lucas scooted his chair back. The rains had finally stopped. It was time for him to take his bedroll back under the stars.

Don't think about stars, he warned himself, but he did anyway. Mandy's skin, gleaming with stick-on stars, was more real to him than Steve and Angel sitting in the kitchen not two feet away.

"Where are you going?" Steve said.

"I'm leaving. You two need your privacy."

"Back to sleep under the stars, Lucas?" Angel said, softly.

"Yep. Not that I don't enjoy your company, Angel." Lucas grabbed his hat off the peg and rammed it on his head.

"Hold on there a minute, Lucas." Steve gave him that I-see-straight-through-you look. "Isn't it about time for you to take off on your motorcycle?"

"The weather's been so bad, I thought I'd stay around the ranch this year. Anyway, you'll have your hands full with Angel."

Steve splayed his big hands across his wife's stomach. "She's a handful, all right," he teased. "But that doesn't mean I want you hanging around feeling trapped. I'm more than capable of handling everything here." He gave his friend another of those looks. "You might want to head back to the vicinity of this Mrs. Sullivan. Angel would love to sign another book."

"Thunderhorse, you're about as subtle as a Sherman tank. Besides, I'm immune to love." Lucas palmed a couple of blueberry muffins before heading for the door.

"I think I'll head toward California this time—check out the Valley girls."

That was his full intention as he packed his gear. Go to California and find a skinny blonde who could obliterate Mandy from his mind. He climbed aboard his GoldWing and headed hopefully west.

Josie and Myrtle had their hands in yeast dough when Mandy walked into the shop wearing a hot pink maternity top and jeans with a stretch panel over the belly. They stopped mid-knead to stare.

"Yes, I'm pregnant," Mandy said. "I'm not married. And I don't intend to be. Any questions?"

"It's none of my business." Myrtle meant what she said. Splinters driven under her nails wouldn't make her tell about Mandy.

"Oh, honey." Josie teared up as she put her arms around Mandy. "A love child! That's about the most romantic thing I've ever heard. Now don't you worry about a thing. I'll help you take care of that baby. We all will, won't we Myrtle?" Myrtle nodded, already busy again with the yeast dough.

"And if anybody says a word to me about you, I'll punch their lights out." Josie took her place at the table and attacked the dough as if it were one of Mandy's future detractors.

"Thank you, both. You have no idea how much your support means to me."

"How did the children take it?" Josie asked.

"Great. They're as excited as I am."

It was true. "We're having a baby," she'd told them the previous night, quickly forestalling inevitable questions, especially from Rusty who was the only one of her children old enough to wonder about the father. "Just the four of us, five counting Grandma. All for one and one for all, right?''

Betsy wanted to know if it would be a girl, and Rusty had snorted, ''Of course not. God's gonna send a boy just like me, and I'm gonna teach him how to carve a whistle.''

He'd gone to school this morning whistling, and Jill and Betsy were jumping up and down with excitement to tell their friends.

Mandy hadn't issued any warnings. It was better to let them announce the news in a joyous and natural way than to tell them to keep quiet, and then have them be the brunt of jokes and teasing.

Mandy was going to handle loose talk by doing all the telling herself, then giving them a look that double-dog-dared them to make snide remarks.

With that plan in mind, she told everybody who came into the bakery, ''I have the most wonderful news. I'm pregnant.'' Then to be certain the word spread, she paraded down Main Street, the only street that amounted to anything in Saltillo, and stopped people on the sidewalk to share her joy.

Conversation came to a halt when she walked into Sally's Café. ''I'm going to have a baby, and I'm celebrating,'' she announced to one and all. Then she gave her biggest smile to show that she meant every word she said.

''Well, congratulations, Mandy. I didn't know you were married.'' There was thinly veiled malice behind Sally's well wishes.

''I'm not, Sally,'' Mandy said, then she sailed right up to the middle of the café, took the center table and ordered the biggest cheeseburger on the menu. ''I love being pregnant," she announced, loud enough for every-body to hear. "Mainly because I get to eat for two."

The laughter dispelled the tension, and that night Mandy lay in her bed with her hands cradling her ex-panding womb.

"We got through the first day, little one," she whis-pered. And then she began to hum. It was only when she realized it was the love song from *Carousel* that Mandy began to cry.

Things went along fine for weeks, and then the inev-itable happened: Rusty came home from school and said that Johnny Clayton had called his mother a tramp and he'd bloodied his nose. Mandy thanked him for defend-ing her honor, then explained to him that there were bet-ter ways to settle matters of that sort.

She explained to her children that people are often rid-iculed because they are different, or because they're un-conventional and have made choices that other people don't approve of.

"We will hold our heads high and be proud," she'd told them, then her mother had added, "Sticks and stones can break your bones, but words can never hurt you. Remember that, children."

Sometimes Evelyn Sullivan made her so proud that her heart hurt. Mandy was putting Mrs. Glover Graham's cake in a box for a two o'clock pickup and thinking about her mother when the bell over the shop door tinkled.

"Just a minute," she said.

"Take your time. I'll wait."

Mandy froze. That voice. It couldn't be. She held her breath, her back to the door. *Make it not be him,* she silently prayed, but the back of her neck began to prickle, and she knew her prayers were in vain.

Lucas Gray Wolf was standing in her shop.

Oh, Lord, I'm going to faint, she thought. Then, *I think I might die.*

She couldn't turn around. She didn't dare. Where were Myrtle and Josie when she needed them? Then she remembered, Wednesday was their afternoon off. Any fool looking beyond the display case could see that the kitchen was empty.

"You're looking good, Mandy."

Every atom in her body came alive. He was Wolf and she was his Lady bird, flying straight to the stars. Mandy's hands trembled so that the box rattled. She squeezed them tightly around the box, then held her breath for a slow count of ten.

"Aren't you going to turn around?"

Blood roared in her ears, and her heart was pumping so hard she worried about the baby.

"I've come a long way for the sight of your face, Lady."

"Don't call me pet names." She fiddled with the box, buying time. "You've lost that right."

"I've come to claim it back."

Did he know about the baby? Had he found out somehow? Had her mother called, after all? Why else would he be here?

Mandy did some quick mental calculations. Although the display case was glass, it was chest high and filled with cookies, cakes, pies and breads. Hopefully, it would camouflage her condition. Especially if she held the cake box in front of her.

Slowly she turned to face Lucas. He was so glorious looking he took her breath away.

"Hello, Mandy."

His deep, rich voice started a tremor in her heart that

vibrated throughout her body. *Lucas, my beloved,* she thought, and then she felt the flutter. A tiny kick against the walls of her womb. The baby's first movement.

You know your father, don't you, little one.

"What can I do for you, Lucas?" she asked, all business, the cake box clutched tightly in front of his unborn child. It was the wrong choice of words. His face lit with such wicked pleasure that Mandy blushed.

"You know what you can do for me, Mandy. You've always known."

Memory colored her face. Memory and fury.

"How dare you march in here after all these months and act as if you never left. You *left,* Lucas. Whatever I did for you, and whatever we had together is over. It's finished."

"I thought so, too. I thought I could drive you out of my mind with somebody else, Mandy. I thought I could outrun my memories by heading to California." His smile was enough to shake her resolve, but it was his eyes, deepened by the color of love, that broke her heart. "I never made it past the Arizona border, Mandy. I turned around and headed back to you."

The thought of him with somebody else almost blinded her with rage. "You slept with another woman?"

"No, I didn't sleep with another woman. There's been no one since you, Mandy."

"But that's what you said."

"You're shouting."

"I'm not shouting." She was, of course. She blamed it on her pregnancy. "And don't you try to make this about *me*. You're the one who left. You're the one who came back expecting…"

Mandy ran out of steam. She held onto the cake box with one hand and ran her other through her hair. She was so hot she was dripping with sweat. That, too, was all his fault.

"Expecting what, Mandy?" His voice was soft and seductive. Oh, he was a clever one all right, trying to soften her up with memories.

He wasn't going to get by with it. She put the ugliest spin she could think of on their beautiful, miraculous love feast in the woods.

"A romp in the hay," she said, putting as much ice into her voice as she could.

"Is that what it was to you, Mandy? A romp in the hay?"   ·

She'd always hated lying. Chuck had told her she was terrible at it. She clutched the cake box so hard her knuckles turned white.

"A one-night stand. A fling. Whatever you want to call it. We both knew going in that's what it was, Lucas. And that's the way we both wanted it."

"Maybe I've changed my mind. Maybe I've come back to try and change yours."

"*Maybe?* You expect me to climb onto the back of your motorcycle and go riding off into the woods so you can discover if *maybe* you've changed your mind? You expect me to drop everything just because you came to Mississippi instead of going to California?"

This wouldn't do. She was close to tears. Pregnant women had volatile emotions. Everybody knew that.

Everybody except Lucas. He still hadn't mentioned the baby. That meant he didn't know. Or it could mean that he was simply being cagey. Or worse, that he didn't care.

Dear Lord in heaven, why did he have to come back?

"You expect me to climb in the sack with you as if the past five months of separation didn't even exist?" she said.

Lucas had retreated into a deep silence, his face as impassive as a mountain. What was she going to do?

"Let me see now, Lucas. Did I miss anything?"

"You have it all figured out, don't you, Mandy? You think you know me well, don't you?"

His eyes did things to her that ought to be declared illegal. He moved forward—Gray Wolf, silently stalking. Shivers went through her. He was so close now she could see his beard shadow.

He was at the edge of the display case, then almost around the corner. Alarm propelled her to action.

"Stop." She held out one arm, stiff as a traffic cop. "You can't come back here."

"What's the matter, Mandy. Afraid of my touch?"

"No." *Yes.* "Regulations. Customers aren't allowed behind the counter."

"I'm not here as a customer," he said, but he stopped, then retreated.

Two more feet and he'd have been around the corner, viewing her from a side angle, the one that made her look as if she'd swallowed a pumpkin. She eased down to the opposite end of the display case where three-layer cakes made a solid wall between her and Lucas.

"You know why I'm here, Mandy."

His voice was softly seductive, designed to make her melt. Well, he'd succeeded. She wanted him more than ever before. She longed for him. She *yearned.*

To be in his arms would be heaven.

Mandy sighed. There was only so much torture she could take. If she didn't get him out of her shop soon, there was no telling what she would do.

"I don't want you here, Lucas," she said. "I don't want to see you. I don't want to be with you. Not now. Not ever."

"Are you sure about that?"

"Yes." *No!* "I'm positive. Leave, Lucas."

Why didn't he say something? He was as silent as a sphinx, looking at her the way he had after they'd made love for the first time, as if she were something precious, breakable.

"Please, Lucas," she whispered.

"I could never deny you anything, Lady." There was enough tenderness in his voice to break a stone, a will, a heart.

He headed to the door. Trembling with relief, Mandy pressed her hot forehead against the cool glass countertop and closed her eyes. She was so tired she could barely move.

"Mandy." She jerked upright. Lucas filled the doorway, blocked out all the light. His eyes burned through her like blue hot flames. "There's something about you...you're more beautiful than I remember...I just wanted to tell you that."

She gave him a wan smile. It was all she could manage.

Please go. Please stay. Dear Lord in heaven, she was so confused she didn't know what to do.

"There's something else I want to tell you, Mandy. I'll be back."

The shop bell tinkled as the door shut behind him and Mandy burst into tears. She didn't care if the Mayor of Saltillo saw her. She didn't care if the Governor of Mississippi saw her. She didn't care who saw her, as long as it wasn't Lucas.

Lucas knew he'd made a mess of things with Mandy. And was it any wonder? He wasn't even sure, himself, why he had come back to Saltillo. How could he expect to explain things to her? All he knew is that somewhere near the Arizona state line he'd known he wasn't going to California. He'd known there was only one place he could go, only one woman he wanted to see. *Desperately* wanted to see.

And that's why he'd driven day and night, without sleep and with very little food until he finally reached Saltillo.

God, Mandy was so beautiful she broke his heart. She positively glowed.

As he headed his GoldWing out of town he thought about how she'd looked standing behind that glass display case—as serene as a Madonna, even when that redhead's temper of hers flared.

Would things have worked out differently if he'd made a flowery speech, if he'd said all the right words? How could he possibly articulate his feelings to Mandy when he didn't even know what they were?

He was too tired to think. The sign up ahead said Lake Lamar Bruce. Lucas took it. There was bound to be a wooded spot where he could pitch camp and get some sleep.

He'd decide what to do about Mandy tomorrow.

The nights had turned cool enough so that sitting on the front porch in the evening was Mandy's favorite pastime. Tonight, it served another purpose, too: it provided privacy for the long talk she was having with her mother.

Lately, Rusty had developed X-ray hearing. Every time Mandy and her mother started a private conversation, he appeared, even late at night when he was supposed to be in bed asleep.

"Lucas is back in town." Mandy set the swing a-sway

with her right foot, doing her best to appear unruffled by this latest development.

Evelyn heaved a long sigh, then swiveled so she could see her daughter's face.

"I don't suppose he came back to marry you?"

"He came back for another fling."

"Is that what he said?"

"Well, not in so many words, but I wasn't born yesterday. I can read between the lines. Besides, I wouldn't marry him, even if he wanted me to. Even if he begged me on bended knees."

"Mandy, *Mandy*..." Evelyn gave another dramatic sigh. "I suppose you think I called him."

"Did you?"

"No, I didn't, but not because I didn't want to. He's that baby's *father,* Mandy. You keep forgetting that."

As if to back up Evelyn's sentiments, the baby kicked hard. Mandy caressed her stomach, feeling the little lumps and bumps that was her baby. Lucas's baby.

She felt like crying again, and so she did. Silently, Evelyn put an arm around Mandy.

"What can I do to help you?" she asked.

"If he comes to the house, don't let him in."

"Maybe if the two of you sat down somewhere quiet and had a long talk, you might work things out."

Mandy jerked herself loose. "Work what out, Mother? A shotgun wedding? Another miserable marriage?"

"How do you know it would be that way? Lucas seemed like such a nice man. It might turn out to be something wonderful."

Something wonderful. There was a song by that name from *The King and I.* Mandy imagined how it would be to cuddle with Lucas in front of the fire while he caressed her distended belly and sang to her and their unborn child.

"I can't bear to think of that right now, Mother. It's all I can do to get through the day."

She thought of the confrontation with him in her shop. He'd promised to come back. What if customers were there? She couldn't make a scene in front of them. And she couldn't lock the door to keep him out.

There was only one thing to do.

"In the morning I'm going to call Josie's niece to see if she can relieve me at the shop for a few days. I need the rest."

There was another long silence.

"Time for bed," Evelyn said, standing up. Then she smoothed her skirt and patted her hair. It was a ritual with her. "Lucas didn't strike me as the kind of man to give up."

"Eventually he will." *I hope. Or do I?*

After her mother left, Mandy stretched out in the swing and leaned her head against one of the patchwork pillows her grandmother Bailey had made. Where was Lucas now? Was he sleeping under the stars?

Mandy looked up into the sky where Venus twinkled.

"Star light, star bright, wish I may, wish I might, have the wish I wish tonight."

The trouble was, she didn't know what to wish for.

Chapter Fourteen

"I'm looking for Mandy."

One of the large women Lucas had glimpsed in the kitchen last summer was standing behind the display case. She didn't bat an eye when he asked for Mandy, didn't change expression, didn't even move. She reminded Lucas of one of those figures in wax museums.

"I'll get Josie." Her mouth barely moved when she spoke, and then she scurried into the kitchen where she hid her face with her hand and engaged in earnest conversation with the other woman, apparently Josie, all the while cutting her eyes toward Lucas.

He caught a phrase every now and then—"that Indian…she didn't say so, but…father of…" They lowered their voices to whispers.

Somebody must have seen the two of them together last summer or else Mandy must have said something to them. Since he was probably the only Sioux for six states, he wouldn't be hard to pick out in Saltillo, even in a crowd.

He tried to look nonchalant, but he had visions of those two generously sized women rushing out with tar and feathers. After all, he was in a small town in the Deep South. They weren't used to savages taking their women captive.

As usual, he was hiding his discomfort behind humor. The women were still talking. Lucas pretended an interest in doughnuts.

Finally, the other woman emerged. She was more jovial looking than the first one.

"Hi, I'm Josie. What can I get for you today?"

"I'll take a dozen doughnuts." Lucas was furious with himself for playing her game. He blamed it on fatigue. Even as exhausted as he'd been yesterday, he hadn't slept much last night. Too much on his mind. Too much uncertainty.

What, exactly, was he doing in Saltillo? Other than the obvious. He wanted Mandy. But what was he going to say to her when he saw her?

"That'll be four dollars," Josie said. Then, "You're new in town, aren't you?"

"Visiting. I'm looking for Mandy. Is she here today?"

"No."

Lucas thanked her, then headed to the door, disappointed. Given his choice, he'd rather have faced Mandy in her shop than at her house under the nose of her mother.

"Uh, Mr....uh..." Josie called after him.

"Gray Wolf," he said. "Lucas Gray Wolf."

"My, isn't that a nice name?" Two bright spots of color dotted Josie's cheeks. "I want you to know, Mr. Gray Wolf, that we're all just as pleased as punch."

Lucas didn't have the foggiest notion what she was talking about. Nor was he going to hang around and find out. He had more important things to do than chat with a sweet old lady about doughnuts.

Outside once more, he tossed the bag of doughnuts into his knapsack, then turned his GoldWing in the direction of Mandy's house.

She heard him coming. There was no way to miss the distinctive roar of a motorcycle, certainly not one as large as Lucas's.

Mandy stood at the window, one hand over her belly, the other twisting the curtain into a wad. He looked like a warrior entering her front yard. A beautiful, black-suited warrior with a take-no-prisoners attitude.

Her heart pounded like a trip-hammer, and the baby landed a hard kick under her ribs. "Mother," Mandy called. "Mother!"

There was no answer. Outside, Lucas parked the bike under a magnolia tree, then strode toward the house. Panicked, Mandy raced toward the kitchen.

"Mother? Where are you?"

"Land sakes!" Evelyn emerged from the pantry, sweaty and disheveled. "Can't a body straighten the pickle jars without all this ruckus? What in the world's the matter with you, Mandy?"

"It's Lucas. He's here." Mandy ducked into the pantry. "Tell him I'm not here."

Evelyn pursed her lips. "I don't like lying."

"Please, just this once. I can't let him see me like this." She rubbed her child-swollen belly.

"It's not like you to hide, Mandy."

"Well, this is different." The doorbell chimed. Mandy frantically waved her hands at her mother. "Hurry,

Mother, before he comes storming in here like a herd of buffalo.''

When Evelyn was mad, she tapped her heels smartly against the floor so everybody would know it. Mandy could hear her all the way to the front door.

Breathing a sigh of relief, she closed herself into the pantry, then got such an attack of claustrophobia she almost swooned. Hastily, she opened the door a crack. She had to have air.

"Hello, Mrs. Sullivan. How are you?"

Lucas oozed charm. Mandy said a silent prayer that her mother wouldn't be swayed.

"Well, my goodness. Look who's here."

Mandy grinned. Her mother had always fancied herself an actress.

"You're looking lovely today. I hope you got the books Angel signed."

"I most certainly did. Thank you very much."

"I stopped by the shop but I didn't see Mandy. I was hoping she'd be here."

"You just missed her. What a shame."

Bravo, Mother. A small stab of guilt smote Mandy. She wished she could see Lucas's face. Did she dare risk cracking the door wider? *No,* she decided. That would be playing with fire.

"I probably should have called first. I hope you don't think I'm rude, barging in like this."

"Oh, no, not at all. You're a gentleman through and through. In fact, I think you're the nicest man Mandy's ever met."

Mandy groaned. What was her mother trying to do?

"Thank you, Mrs. Sullivan. That compliment means a great deal, coming from you."

''The children feel the same way. They still talk about you, especially Rusty.''

''I'd like to see them while I'm here.''

''Do you plan to stay long, Lucas?''

Mandy cracked the door wider so she wouldn't miss what he said.

''I'm staying as long as it takes to get your daughter to talk to me, Mrs. Sullivan.''

Confusion tore Mandy apart. Hiding in the pantry, she was equal parts anger, triumph, anxiety and hope. *How dare he?* she silently fumed. Quick on the heels of that thought came another: *See there, I knew he wouldn't leave.* Then, *What am I going to do? I can't hide forever.*

The small glimmer of hope was the most heartbreaking of all. *He loves me,* a still, small voice inside her head whispered. But she knew it wasn't so. Was it? If he loved her, he would say so, wouldn't he?

All Mandy had ever wanted out of life was to have a family of her own, lots of babies and a good man who loved her. Some folks would chide her for not having more ambition. Some would accuse her of wasting her talents, whatever they were. Some would say that women nowadays can have it all—career, children, a great marriage.

Some of them did. She knew that. But in Mandy's opinion having a loving family was *having it all.* Why would she want to wear herself out working eight to twelve hours a day in the bakery, then come home so tired she didn't feel like romping with the children, let alone being sexy and carefree with her husband.

If she had a husband.

Mandy was going to cry again. Not one of those quiet sessions where the tears rolled silently down her cheeks and one handkerchief was enough to control her nose. No, she felt a self-indulgent deluge coming on.

And she was trapped inside with the dills and the pickled peaches and the tomato relish, peeking through a crack in the door at a man who still had the power to drive her over-the-moon crazy with desire.

She could see only his profile as he sat unmoving on the swing, but it was enough. She wanted him as she'd never wanted another man. Besides that, tenderness swamped her when she looked at him. He was in her heart as surely as his baby was in her womb.

He would always be in her heart, no matter what happened.

"Can I get you something to drink, Lucas?"

Mandy cringed. *Why, Mother?*

"That would be great."

He was out of the swing so fast it rocked like the tilt-o-twirl at the carnival. The next thing Mandy knew he'd be storming through the front door and jerking open the pantry door. She'd as soon face a firing squad.

She beat a hasty retreat, misjudging both the distance to the shelves and her size. Pickle jars rocked and swayed, tomato relish tangoed, and a quart jar of pear preserves crashed to the floor.

Now she'd done it.

"What was that?" Lucas said, and suddenly he was looking right at her. At least, that's the way it felt. With the door barely open and all that distance between them, surely he didn't see her, and yet Mandy knew he did. She could tell because of the prickles at the back of her neck. Maybe he saw her upper arm or her leg or the outline of her cheek.

He *saw.* Furthermore, he *knew.*

Too late, Mandy shut the door. If she died of claustrophobia it would be all his fault.

The front door opened and shut, footsteps tapped on the floor. Her mother. Evelyn's mad march again. She listened for Lucas, but couldn't hear him.

Why should she? He was Sioux, he was silent, he was probably angrier than a wet hen.

"Mandy?" It was her mother, standing outside the pantry door hissing like a snake. "Are you all right?"

"Where's Lucas?" Mandy whispered.

"On the front porch. I'm getting him some iced tea."

"Get rid of him."

Her mother didn't answer. Mandy heard the refrigerator door open, then shut. She heard ice tinkle against glass, then her mother tap-tapping toward the front porch. The screen door popped, and then there was silence.

What were they saying? What was Lucas doing? Mandy didn't dare open the door. She felt something sticky on her leg. Blood or pear preserves? She didn't dare move. There was glass all over the floor. If she didn't cut herself, she was bound to go down in the slippery mess.

It was dark in the closet, and she was getting a cramp in her left leg. Besides that, she needed to go to the bathroom. She needed a drink of water. She was getting nauseated. She needed a cracker.

Sweat inched down the side of her face, then trickled down the front of her blouse. What time was it? How much longer was he going to stay?

"Mandy." Her mother's sharp voice made her jump. "You can come out now."

"Has Lucas gone?"

"Yes, more's the pity." Mandy opened the door and

Evelyn pursed her mouth so tightly it practically disappeared. She surveyed the damage in stoic silence.

"I'll clean it, up," Mandy said.

"Not in your condition. You're liable to hurt yourself." Evelyn got paper towels, a mop and a bucket, then set to work. "I don't like telling lies," she said.

"I know. I'm sorry, Mother."

"You ought to be." Evelyn scrubbed with a vengeance. "Lying to a nice man like that. You're making a mistake, Mandy."

Mandy poured herself a tall glass of ice water, then sank into a chair to inspect her legs. They were spattered with pear preserves, and there was a small scratch from a glass shard. A Band-Aid would cover the damage.

"As soon as I clean my legs, I'm going to pick up Jill at the nursery." She got no response from Evelyn. "Mother, did you hear me?"

"I heard you." Evelyn set aside her mop and leaned against the pantry door. "He said he was staying till you talked to him. I want to know what you're going to do when he comes back."

"I'll cross that bridge when I come to it."

Evelyn started to comment, then pursed her lips and turned back to mopping, letting her unrelenting posture do the talking for her.

After Mandy had cleaned herself up, she stood at her bedroom window searching for signs of Lucas. Like a spy. Like a prisoner in her own house. Like a coward.

"I can't hide forever," she whispered. Besides, hiding was not her style. If she persisted she was going to lose more than her pride—she was liable to lose her business. Josie's niece was no substitute for Mandy, and while Josie and Myrtle were good cooks and hard workers, they didn't understand the business end of the bakery.

Seeing that the coast was clear, Mandy went downstairs and backed her car out of the garage. By the time she'd pulled onto the street she was leading with her chin again.

She was through with hiding. Tonight she was going to the bakery to catch up on that big order for Margaret Jones's party, and tomorrow she was going about her business in a normal fashion.

Lucas or no Lucas.

Mandy had been in the house. Lucas knew that. He'd known from the minute he set foot on her porch. The crash in the vicinity of the kitchen confirmed it. That's one reason he'd stayed so long. If she was going to hide from him, let her suffer.

Viciously, he revved his bike into a law-breaking speed. He needed some fresh air. He needed to clear his head.

He roared past the city-limits sign, then raced along the country roads till hunger drove him back to town. It was dark by the time Saltillo came into view, and he stopped at the first restaurant he saw. A place by the name of Sally's Café.

"What can I do for you, hon?" It was Sally herself, sporting a name tag decorated with jack-o'-lanterns.

Lucas scanned the menu, then ordered country fried steak. When Sally brought his order, she didn't leave, but propped her hands on her hips and looked him over the way he did the horses he bought for Paradise Ranch.

"You're new in town, aren't you?"

He made it a point never to tell anybody his business. But in this case, he decided to make an exception. This was Mandy's hometown, and a small one at that. Maybe he could learn something about her.

"Yes," he said. "I'm visiting Mandy Belinda. Maybe you know her."

"Mandy? Lord, everybody knows her. She's a card."

Whatever that meant. Lucas didn't ask. In fact, he didn't have to say a thing, because Sally was still at his table, lighting up a cigarette and in the mood to talk, if he was any judge.

"Matter of fact, she was in here a minute ago, grabbed a cheeseburger and fries to take back to work."

Bingo. Mandy was at the bakery. Lucas picked up his fork, hoping Sally would take the hint, but she was still at his table, still talking.

"She's a sight, that girl is. Lord, you should'a been here when she announced her pregnancy."

Lucas felt as if stakes had been driven into his heart. *Mandy? Pregnant?*

"Nobody but Mandy Sullivan Belinda could pull off being an unwed mother with such pizzazz."

Sally was looking at Lucas, expecting a comment, so he mumbled, "Nobody but Mandy."

He was numb with shock, with awe, with love, with rage.

"How d'you know her, hon?"

Intimately. Lucas stared at his food, still dazed. There was no way he was going to be able to eat it.

Sally was still waiting for his answer. In fact, so was everybody else in the café. *Mandy had announced her pregnancy, had she?* He could see why.

"How do I know her?" Lucas shoved his food aside and stood up. "I'm the father," he announced, then walked out in the midst of stunned silence. When he reached the door, though, somebody started clapping.

Soon everybody joined in, and Lucas made his exit to thunderous applause.

Mandy would surely kill him.

If he didn't kill her first.

Chapter Fifteen

A row of lemon cream pies stood on a shelf, and next to them, the cherry pies. Chocolate cakes cooled on racks and lemon chiffon layers were lined up waiting for the lemon sugar icing Mandy was mixing.

She loved working at night by herself. There was nobody around to bother her, no customers ringing the shop bell, no children demanding bedtime stories. She did her best thinking in the kitchen with her hands busy, and what she was thinking made her grimace.

She had to face Lucas. That's all there was to it. Tomorrow she would find him before he found her. The element of surprise would give her some small advantage. And when she found him she'd tell him in no uncertain terms to leave her alone. She'd say she didn't need him, didn't want him, and didn't intend to have him. She'd say, *pack up and get out of town,* or words to that effect.

Her knees got weak thinking about that confrontation. It certainly wasn't one she relished. Obviously, he would notice her condition.

She didn't know what she'd say about that, but she'd be willing to bet that he would say plenty. Mandy sighed. Wiping her hands on a dish towel, she rubbed her back, then because she wanted to, she cradled her child-heavy belly.

"It's going to be all right, little one," she crooned. "All for one and one for all. You'll see."

She caressed her abdomen, loving the shape and feel of it. As always, the thought of her baby made her smile.

Suddenly, she was alert. Was that a shadow at the window?

"Who's there?" she called. "Is anybody there?"

This wasn't the first time she'd worked alone at night, and she certainly wasn't scared. Not in Saltillo. One of the things she loved about this town was the strong sense of community, the sense of hometown pride, the sense that her neighbors not only knew her but cared about her.

She was being silly. That was all. Pregnant women were entitled.

Humming softly, Mandy sank her hands into the sugar icing and went back to work.

The pounding on the back door startled her. Had something happened to one of the children? Without even wiping her hands, Mandy raced to the door. It rattled with a second onslaught of pounding.

What was her mother using? A sledgehammer?

"Mother?" Mandy already had her hands on the doorknob when her unexpected visitor answered, "No, it's me." *Lucas.* Mandy backed away, her heart hammering.

"I know you're in there, Mandy. Open up."

What was she going to do? Her door wasn't made to withstand the terrible beating he was inflicting on it.

"Mandy, you can't keep me out. If you don't open up I'm going to kick this door down."

She'd never seen Lucas this way. What was the matter with him?

"Mandy!" The door strained at its hinges.

"Just a minute. I'm coming."

The pounding ceased. Pressing her hands over her belly, Mandy drew a deep breath. It didn't help her one bit. Lucas was outside her door, and nothing was going to help her.

Sending a prayer winging upward, Mandy swung the door open.

He stood there staring at her, his eyes so hot and glittering they made her shiver. Mandy wrapped her arms tightly around herself, but there was not a thing she could do to camouflage her condition. Carried high and proud, Lucas's unborn baby dominated the view.

Mandy held her breath, waiting for him to speak. Instead, he stalked into the shop and locked the door behind him.

Mandy wet her dry lips with the tip of her tongue. "Lucas?" The look in his eyes made her take a step backward.

"When were you going to tell me, Mandy?"

So, he wanted a fight? Well, she was willing to give it to him. More than willing. In fact, she was itching to give it to him, and had been, she realized, ever since she'd discovered she was pregnant.

"I wasn't. You got what you came for last summer, then you left me to pick up the pieces. Go back to Arizona, Lucas, and leave me alone."

"That's *my* baby you're carrying. *My child.*"

"This is my body and my baby. Your being the father is merely a biological accident."

Lucas closed in. Her first instinct was to back away, but Mandy was sick and tired of playing the coward with him. Chin up, back straight and proud, she stood her ground.

Let's see how close you come, Lucas. Closer than she expected. Lucas came so close he was almost touching the front of her big belly.

"Do you want to know how I found out, Mandy?" His voice was deceptively soft, a steel blade sheathed in satin.

"This is a small town. People talk."

"They certainly do." The coldness in his smile made her shiver. "I gave them something else to talk about."

Mandy refused to rise to the bait. She'd been the talk of the town for months. What else was there to say about her?

His eyes sought—then held—hers. Mandy met him stare for stare, then wished she hadn't. There was a subtle shifting in him, a softening she could see in his eyes. For an instant they reminded her of the way Lucas had looked in the cave when he'd painted her skin with wings, then made love to her in the midst of a rainbow.

Lucas, my darling, my love.

How many times could a heart break?

With all her being she wanted to touch him, wanted him to touch her. If she had the power to rearrange events, she would go back to that crystal cave, back to Lucas's arms, and at the moment he spilled his seed she would cry out her love for him. She would say it simply. *I love you, Lucas.* And then he would know. For all time, Lucas Gray Wolf would know that the child she carried had been conceived in love. He would know that no matter what happened, Mandy carried him in her heart. Forever.

She couldn't say those things now. It was far, far too late.

Slowly, Lucas stretched his hand downward, toward her stomach. Mandy held her breath. He was so close she could feel the heat that pulsed from his hand. Could her baby feel it too? Did he know his father was near?

The connection between the mother and her fetus was so powerful, the baby responded to her thoughts. *Yes,* he told her with a vigorous kick, *Yes, I know.*

Lucas's hand trembled above her womb. She longed to hold it against her belly and say, "Feel that, feel how strong your child is."

"Lucas…" Mandy stopped herself from giving soft explanations. Nothing could erase the long, lonely months, the pain of knowing he'd used her, the agony of realizing he'd returned for the same reason.

He jerked his hand back as if it were on fire, and his face became a cold mask. This was not the Lucas Gray Wolf she'd known and loved.

"I heard about my child from strangers, Mandy. Sally told me, as well as everybody else in the café who didn't already know."

It was bound to happen sooner or later. Why hadn't Mandy foreseen that? Why hadn't she told him the first day? Then they both would have been spared this pain.

There was no mistaking the hurt in his eyes.

"I'm sorry, Lucas," she said. "I didn't mean for you to find out this way. I didn't mean for you to find out at all."

"You meant to keep my child from me." It was not a question. It was a statement, spoken in a tone that would freeze blood. Hearing it from Lucas made her feel small and vindictive, like a spiteful woman who was getting back at the man responsible for her condition.

"It's not like that, Lucas."

"You're right, Mandy. It's not going to be like that. I'm the father of this baby, and soon everybody in town will know. Like you, I announced the good news in Sally's Café."

Disbelief and rage warred in Mandy. Rage won. She threw the first thing she could get her hands on, which turned out to be a cherry pie. It splatted on the wall behind his head, and while the red stain was still spreading she reached for another. Then she took dead aim at his crotch.

Lucas had never known a woman who could go so quickly from softness to anger. Which proved to be a very good thing. If she hadn't thrown that pie there's no telling what he would have done.

The sight of her pregnant had taken his breath away. Standing outside her window watching her, flush-faced and heavy with his child, he'd almost cried.

Close-up, it had been worse. The temptation to touch her had been so great, and he trembled with the effort to keep his hands to himself.

"How dare you," she yelled, then lobbed another pie, straight at the front of his pants. He had the reflexes of a cat, thanks to years of dodging the flying hooves of wild ponies.

That's what Mandy reminded him of now, one of the wild ponies he'd seen up in the canyons near the ranch, kicking up a storm at the least little threat, and sometimes snorting and cavorting simply for the fun of it.

She was reaching for another pie.

"Mandy, stop that." His voice didn't even register through her rage.

She scooped up two lemon cream pies and let him have it with both barrels. The first whizzed past his head, but the second caught him in the chest.

"Your aim's getting better."

"Are you laughing at me? I'll show you."

She cleared the top shelf with one swoop, sending cream pies flying. Yellow custard and whipped cream spattered his boots and dotted his pants. Globs of it clung to Mandy's hands and arms, and speckles decorated her red hair.

She was heaving with effort. "Isn't it enough that I've been the brunt of gossip for months? You have to add to it?"

Remorse slashed through Lucas, but there was no turning back now. The deed was done. Furthermore, he wasn't about to lose sight of the facts: Mandy was carrying his child, and she intended to deprive him of his rights as a father.

"All you had to do was call me, Mandy. I would have come."

"I'd be put in stocks in the town square before I'd be a ball and chain."

With another swipe she cleared the second shelf. Cherry pie filling washed across the floor like a pool of blood.

"Stop that, Mandy. You're going to hurt yourself."

"What do you care?"

Out of pies, she started toward the mixing bowl. Her feet slipped in cherries, and her arms windmilled as she tried for balance.

Gripped by terror, Lucas lunged. She fell heavily against him, and he almost lost his footing.

I'm going to lose both of them, he thought, and it was the first real terror he'd known since he stood in the woods and watched the fires.

"Hang on, Mandy. I've got you."

He prayed it was true. Her changed body was rammed up against him, and even as he sought purchase for his feet he marveled at the way her breasts had ripened for his child and at the heavy mound of her womb. In spite of her growing girth, she still felt slender to him, vulnerable and extremely fragile. He was scared to hold her too close lest he wound her somehow, lest he endanger his baby.

His baby. He was going to be a father. The concept was awesome to him. He felt some deep primeval urge to make a pilgrimage into the home of his ancestors and pay homage to the Father Creator in the ancient Sioux way.

Holding onto Mandy with one hand, he caught the edge of the table with his other, anchoring them with a firm grip and sheer willpower. When he was steady against the table, he held her tenderly, soothing her with soft murmurings and gentle caresses.

She made little snuffling noises against his chest, and he knew she was crying. Lucas silently damned himself for being the cause of her tears. He cursed himself for taking her into the woods last summer and not taking precautions.

And yet, there was a deep wellspring of joy in him, of pride and pleasure at the thought of the tiny being he'd sired. With startling clarity he knew what love was. It was total immersion in another. The child was him and he was the child, and he loved it with all his being. He couldn't imagine a time when the baby wasn't growing in Mandy's womb.

The power of love was so great, that his arms trembled as he held her. She burrowed closer, and suddenly he had a vision of how it would be with them if circumstances were different. He would pamper her. He would massage her feet and sing to her in front of a cozy fire and carry her meals on a tray that held a single yellow rose.

Instinctively, he knew that's what she would love— yellow roses.

Maybe he was going about all this the wrong way, roaring back into her life, making demands. Maybe if he courted her with yellow roses...

Mandy jerked away from him and started toward a chair. She tried to swat him away, but he held onto her arm anyhow.

"You don't want to fall. You might harm the baby."

He saw himself as being solicitous and kind, but she took it the wrong way.

"That's all you care about, isn't it? The baby."

Was it? He was already tempting the fates by loving his unborn child beyond all reason. He didn't dare add to the temptation by declaring love for Mandy...if that's what his feelings were. A stranger to this emotional arena, he didn't know.

"Forget I said that. Forget me. Forget us." Full of wounded disdain she cupped her hands protectively around her stomach. "Just go back to Arizona and leave us alone."

"No. I can't do that."

Tears pooled in her eyes. "Haven't you done enough damage?"

"I didn't throw the pies, Mandy," he said, deliberately ignoring the subtleties of her accusation. "But I'll clean it up. Where's the mop?"

Thankfully, she didn't argue. Instead she pointed to the

utility closet and Lucas set to work. Mandy stayed in her chair, silent.

Every now and then he would look up from his work and find her watching him with a weary sort of tenderness on her face. Usually, she would look quickly away, but sometimes she held his gaze, and when she did the earth stopped spinning. Everything he valued in the world was contained in that room centered in Mandy's eyes, in Mandy's womb. And it scared him to death.

Finally, the task was done. Lucas had no idea what time it was. He only knew that the moon had started its descent, and he was weary.

Mandy must be exhausted.

"Let me drive you home, Mandy. You need to be in bed."

"Stop it. I don't need you to take care of me. I've been doing it for years and I'll continue doing it."

Fatigue showed in her face, but not in her voice. She was still mad, and her anger rekindled his.

"Let's get something straight, Mandy. I'm going to be a part of my child's life if I have to hound you till my dying days."

"We don't need you, Lucas. Can't you understand that?"

"You're the one who doesn't understand. I grew up an orphan. I know what it's like to be a fatherless, motherless child. My child *will not* be without a father."

Their eyes clashed, and Mandy was the first to look away. She stood up, smoothing her shirt over her bulging abdomen.

"How do you know I don't have somebody else picked out for the job?"

If she was trying to goad him, she was doing a superb

job. Fury propelled him as he stalked her. She backed away, reaching blindly behind her.

Looking for another pie to throw, no doubt.

Lucas scooped her up and marched toward the door. She hammered her fists against his chest.

"Put me down."

He ignored her.

"Where do you think you're going?" He nabbed her purse hanging on the coatrack, then kicked open the back door.

"You put me down this minute or I'll scream."

"Have you ever seen an Indian on the warpath? Go ahead, Mandy. Scream all you like."

She fell silent, but every muscle in her body was rigid. Lucas didn't know about such things, but he was certain that antics like these couldn't be good for the baby.

"I'm taking you home, Mandy," he said, gentling his tone. "I don't want you driving in your condition."

"I'm pregnant, Lucas, not helpless."

"You're angry and much too upset to drive."

"If you think I'm getting on that bike, you're crazy."

He handed her the purse. "Find your keys. We're going in your car."

"What about your bike?"

"Forget the bike. I'll walk back for it."

"That's more than six miles."

"A snap. A breeze. A stroll in the park." An old tune about strolling through the park one day popped into his head and he started singing.

"Shush. Do you want to wake up half of Saltillo?"

"Is that a smile I see?"

"It is not." Mandy made a face at him. "Put me down and drive. I'm sleepy and I want to go to bed."

"Your wish is my command, Lady."

That, too, popped out. The old familiar endearment.
He glanced at Mandy, but she quickly turned her face
toward the window. Lucas flipped on the radio and tried
to focus all his attention on the road, but with Mandy
beside him, such concentration was impossible.

He kept stealing glances at the soft mound of her belly
and thinking of the miracle of birth. Near the city limits
it started to rain. The rhythm of the tires swishing on the
wet highway was mesmerizing.

Suddenly, he felt a soft weight as Mandy slumped
against his shoulder, asleep. Smiling, Lucas put his arm
around her.

Why couldn't she be as nice awake as she was asleep?

Thunderhorse had told him that pregnancy did strange
things to women. At the time Lucas had never dreamed
he'd find out firsthand.

Was it Mandy's pregnancy that made her so ornery, or
was she really so determined to keep him from his child?

The glow from a waning moon fell across her face.
She looked extremely vulnerable in her sleep, and so
beautiful Lucas felt the sting of tears.

Mandy, he whispered. *What's to become of us?*

He parked under the big magnolia tree in her front
yard, then sat in the car holding onto her, reluctant to let
the tender burden go.

He must have dozed a moment, for when he woke up
the moon was only a sliver in a graying sky. Taking care
not to wake her, Lucas slipped from the car, then lifted
Mandy and carried her into the house.

Fortunately, she was not one of those women who carried a dozen keys on her key ring, and he had no trouble
finding the one that opened her front door.

Feeling like a sneak thief, he carried her upstairs and
laid her on the bed. Her face was flushed with the heat

of slumber, and where she'd leaned against him, her hair was damp with sweat.

Lucas smoothed back her hair, then slipped off her shoes. He found a towel and wiped off the custard. She mumbled in her sleep, flung her left arm above her head and sank deeper into her pillow.

Lucas knew he should leave, but he couldn't. Not yet.

He could see the puffy flesh where her shoe straps had cut into her feet. He sat on the edge of the bed and tenderly massaged them.

Mandy made a humming sound of contentment, and for a moment he thought he'd roused her from sleep. He held his breath till she drew a long ragged sigh and her breathing became even again.

The sky had turned a pale pink, and beyond the window he could see a strip of purest gold peeking over the eastern horizon. In the soft light of dawn, Mandy looked like a painting by Reubens, lush and glowing with life.

The changes in her body fascinated him. He thought of the way she'd looked in the woods, covered with stick-on stars. They had been glorious together, soft and tender one minute, wild and hungry the next.

And always, he'd wanted her. She'd been a fire in his blood that he couldn't extinguish, no matter how many times he had her.

Was it any wonder she carried his child?

He placed his hands lightly over the mound of her abdomen, thrilled at the pulsing of life he felt there. He could have stayed like that for hours, for days, but the golden rim of sun widened. Soon it would be morning.

There was one more thing he had to do before he left. Bending down, Lucas placed a soft kiss on her distended belly.

Chapter Sixteen

Mandy woke up at first light. Groaning, she sat up in bed, so tired she felt as if somebody had taken a sledgehammer to her.

What time was it? She glanced at the clock on her bedside table. Six o'clock. Soon the children would be stirring, and she had a million things to do. Make pies, for one.

In the cold light of morning, she regretted having thrown her pies at Lucas. In fact, she regretted many things, among them not telling him about the baby. But never, *never* did she regret being pregnant. Not for one second did she regret having gone to the woods with him.

Mandy reached for a robe, then realized she was still dressed. She groaned again.

"Mandy, are you all right?" It was her mother.

"Yes, I'm fine."

Evelyn came into the bedroom in her chenille robe,

her hair in pink foam curlers. "What in the tarnation are you doing in bed with your dress on?"

"Lucas put me here."

Evelyn beamed. "Well, then, I guess everything's settled. Under the circumstances I think a quiet ceremony at the JP's office would be best."

"There's not going to be a ceremony, Mother. How many times do I have to say that?"

"There's no call for you to be so grouchy. I was never grouchy when I was pregnant." Evelyn polished her glasses. "With Lucas in town it can't be long before the children find out about him being the father and all. Have you thought about that?"

She hadn't. Mandy buried her face in her hands. Didn't she have enough to deal with without that, too?

Evelyn sat down beside her and rubbed her back. "I know you think I'm being stubborn and old-fashioned, Mandy, and Lord knows I'm as thrilled about this baby as you are, and I'll do everything in my power to help you, but there's one thing I want to know."

"What's that, Mother?"

"Do you love him?"

She'd loved him for so long that she couldn't imagine being without those feelings. Loving Lucas was an affirmation of life, a celebration and a prayer, all at the same time. It was like having sunshine on her skin all the time, like having Fourth of July sparklers igniting her heart, like having wings folded just beneath her blouse that gave her the power to fly whenever she took a notion.

"Yes, Mother, I love him, but that's beside the point. I've already told you all the reasons I'll raise this baby without him."

"Still, I can't help but believe you're making a mistake."

It was Mandy's turn to console. "We'll get through this somehow, Mother. I promise you."

"You're a good daughter, Mandy. Did I ever tell you that?"

"Once, I think, when I was in the fourth grade and won the spelling bee."

"Oh, you…" Evelyn swatted her playfully, then fluffed up her hair. "I'd better go put on my face. You never can tell who'll come calling."

She meant Lucas, of course, and that was why Mandy decided the pies could wait. She had far more pressing business to attend to.

Even with the time difference, Lucas didn't have long to wait before calling Paradise Ranch. Steve Thunderhorse was always up before the sun.

"Lucas, what's up?"

"Plenty. I've just discovered I'm going to be a father."

There was a long silence, followed by a barrage of questions. "When did this happen? Who's the woman? Are you sure the child's yours?"

"Last summer, Mandy Belinda, and yes."

Another pause, then Steve chuckled. "You're always trying to steal my thunder. Are you going to marry her?"

"She won't even talk to me. Anyhow, how can I ever trust her? She tried to keep the baby a secret from me. She thinks I'm going to ride off into the sunset and leave my child to her."

"Obviously, she doesn't know you. When's the baby due?"

"I don't know, but I'm going to find out."

"What can I do to help you, pal?"

"Talk to our lawyer. Find out my rights. I'd call but I think it's best done in person."

"You're probably right."

"I'll give you the details. Got a pen handy?"

"Just a minute." Lucas heard Steve scrambling around for pen and paper. "Ready."

Recounting the details of his relationship tore off a chunk of his heart and when Lucas hung up the phone he was raw and bleeding. And getting mad all over again.

He smote the telephone booth with his fist. "Dammit, Mandy, why did you have to do this to us?"

There was the sound of a car engine, and her car hove into sight, as if saying her name had conjured her up. Lucas shaded his eyes and watched her come closer.

She parked beside the phone booth and rolled down her window.

"Lucas, I want to talk to you."

"That's a switch."

Seeing her again so unexpectedly threw Lucas off balance. There were dark circles under her eyes from fatigue, and small smudges of mascara on her cheeks.

Had she been crying? He didn't like to think of her unhappy. *Why not?* he asked himself, but he had no answers.

It had taken him years to put the fires behind him, and after he had, he'd thought he would never again feel the way he had as a child, cast adrift, a lonely sailor without a lifeboat, without even a fixed place in the heavens to guide him.

But that's exactly how he was feeling now. And he didn't like it. Not one bit.

"How did you find me?" The telephone booth had suddenly become a safe haven, and he stayed close, not giving an inch to Mandy.

"I asked myself where would I go if I wanted to stay

around Saltillo, but didn't want to stay in a motel. The lake was the only logical place."

"Bravo, Mandy. You have logic down pat, don't you?"

The hostility in his voice took both of them aback. She winced and Lucas felt like a mangy cur. All his life he'd taken care not to be cruel to another living soul. But Mandy had him breaking all his rules. She always had.

The ache in his heart threatened to destroy him. He left the false safety of the phone booth, and leaned in her window. Then he wished he hadn't.

The mascara on her cheeks was from tear tracks. Lucas wanted to take her in his arms and comfort her. It was always dangerous to comfort an enemy. Even thinking about it was dangerous.

"All right, Mandy, let's go back to my campsite and talk."

A tentative smile trembled on her lips. Fool that he was, he'd addressed her in the soft voice of a lover.

"Do you want to ride with me, Lucas?"

Her artless statement released a flood of memories, and he guessed that what he was thinking showed in his face. Mandy blushed a deep pink.

"In the car, I mean," she said.

"I know what you mean."

The campsite wasn't far. He'd walked to the telephone booth, and if he were smart he'd walk back.

Lucas went around the car and climbed in. Her perfume seduced him. She was gripping the steering wheel hard, and even the sight of her blue-veined wrists aroused him.

Sometimes he wasn't smart.

She cranked the car and he gave her directions, then looked out the window. Would it be so bad being married to her? He'd always considered marriage the antithesis of freedom, and yet Steve didn't feel that way. Since his marriage to Angel, he was happier than he'd ever been.

Still, there were practical considerations. Marriage came with a lot of trappings. Houses, for instance. And where there were houses, there was always the chance of fire and the devastating losses that followed.

His GoldWing came into view and Mandy parked in the shade of a spreading blackjack oak.

"Lucas, I wouldn't have come here this morning except that I want to get a few things straight with you."

Her whole body was rigid, and she was gripping the wheel as if her life depended on it. Besides that, she had the seat so far forward the bottom of the steering wheel poked into her belly and his long legs were twisted like pretzels.

"Let's get out so we'll have more room," he said.

"No. I want to say what I have to say, then leave."

"I thought you wanted to talk."

"I do."

"Conversation is a two-way street." He got out, then went around the car and jerked open her door and held out his hand. "Coming, Mandy?"

"Or what? You'll throw me over your shoulder like you did last night?"

"I didn't throw you over my shoulder. I carried you out like a gentleman."

"You took me captive."

"I'm not going to stand here and argue with you, Mandy."

Without further ado, he scooped her out of the car, then eased her down to his blanket. At the same time, they both realized it was the same blanket they'd used in the woods.

They froze, eyes locked, breath stolen by memories that made them tremble.

Mandy's credo had always been "Nothing can bring me down in flaming defeat." All it took was a split second to prove her wrong. With the rainbow coloured blanket at her back and Lucas bending over her, she saw how it was possible for everything she'd believed to turn upside down. She saw how it was possible that her stance on bringing up her baby was merely a way of camouflaging her fear.

Put plain and simply, she was afraid Lucas wouldn't want her. Why should he? He was bronze and handsome and sexy and carefree, while she was a short, slightly frazzled person with three children and another on the way.

There was only so much rejection a woman could take. She wasn't about to open herself to that again. She was overpowered by Lucas, surrounded by him, overwhelmed by him. She had survived when he left in June. But she didn't think she could survive if she opened her heart to him and he left her again.

And he would, of course. He wasn't the marrying kind. He might try it for a while, for the sake of the baby, but a child wasn't enough to keep a man at her side. Chuck was living proof of that.

But oh, Lucas tempted her so. His eyes were deep blue pools, and she was drowning. And there was nobody to throw her a life jacket.

She gave herself a pep talk. *Well, Mandy, unless you want to end up with a heart broken beyond repair you'd better save yourself.*

"Please," she whispered.

"Please what?"

Oh, God, Lucas was making love to her with his voice,

and she was melting. Soon she'd be nothing but a puddle at his feet, and he'd step all over her.

Mandy shoved his chest. "Get off me. I need air."

To prove her point she took big dramatic gulps, like somebody dying. Instead of sending him away, it brought him closer. Lucas put one hand on her forehead and another on her abdomen, as if she didn't already have enough to drive her crazy.

"Are you all right? Do you need a doctor?"

"For goodness sakes! I'm healthy as a horse. Move off my blanket."

Devilment twinkled in his eyes. "It *is* your blanket, isn't it?"

"You can put that thought right out of your mind."

"What thought?"

"You know. What you were thinking…about me… about this blanket."

"I see you remember."

Rage propelled her to her feet. "Of course I remember." She cupped her swollen belly. "Why in the world shouldn't I? I'm carrying the evidence."

She'd made him mad again, and in a way that was a good thing. They were getting too chummy for her mental health.

"Is that what you call my child? *Evidence?* As if we'd committed some kind of crime?"

"I knew I shouldn't have come here today." She started toward her car, but Lucas blocked her way. They glared at each other like two raging bulls, then all the steam went out of her. Lucas saw it, and was immediately contrite.

"Forgive me, Mandy. I've had less than twenty-four hours to get used to the idea of being a father."

"Okay, Lucas. Truce?"

"Truce."

She sighed, then looked for a place to sit besides the blanket. She'd be darned if she would touch it again. She sat on the picnic bench beside the tree. Lucas didn't move.

"You don't have to guard the car," she said. "I'm not going to bolt."

"I prefer to stand. Go ahead, talk."

"There's no way to get around the fact that you're the father, Lucas, and I should have told you sooner. I know that now." She paused, waiting for him to say something, but he had turned into a wooden Indian, the kind that used to stand on the street beside barber poles staring at customers with hard unblinking eyes out of a face that looked as if it had been carved with a tomahawk.

"I have not changed my mind about raising this baby alone, but I have changed my mind about your being part of his life." She cradled herself, for comfort, mostly. "After the baby is born we'll make some sort of arrangement for you to visit every so often."

He was still silent. She drew a deep breath.

"Until then, I want you to leave Saltillo. I don't want to see you anymore. I don't want my children to know you are here."

He didn't blink, didn't flicker a muscle. She wished he would say something. She wished she could read his face.

A mosquito who didn't know it was October buzzed her head, and a mockingbird scolded a squirrel in the oak tree. Two mallards flew over and made a smooth landing on the lake behind them.

"Marry me, Mandy."

Shock nearly knocked her off the picnic bench. "What?"

"I said, marry me."

"Just like that." She snapped her fingers. "You can't have the baby without the mother, so you propose."

"I didn't say that."

"No, but you didn't say anything else either, Lucas. There are words a woman likes to hear when a man proposes. But then, I don't suppose they're even in your vocabulary."

"You have a stinger, Mandy. I never knew that."

"Well, then, there's another thing. You don't even know me. How can you possibly want to spend the rest of your life with me?" She stood up and arched her back, getting the kinks out. "The answer is *no*, Lucas. The answer will always be no."

"Always?"

She knew better than to make rash statements. But she also knew better than to cling to false hope. Lucas would never say *I love you*. He might want her, but he would never *need* her. He might step in for the short haul, but lifelong commitment was as foreign to him as living in a real house.

She let her silence speak for her.

"That's my answer to your modest proposal, too, Mandy. No."

"No?"

"You heard me. *No.* Redhead or not, you can't order me to leave town. And you certainly can't order me to be nothing more than a part-time father."

"I don't see that you have any choice in the matter, Lucas. Now, will you get out of my way? I'm leaving."

"Running away won't help you, Mandy. I'm going to lay siege to your fort, the likes of which you've never seen."

"Is that a threat?"

"That's a promise."

It was hard to sweep past him looking dignified and elegant when she was as big as a freshening cow, but she tried. Never let it be said that Mandy Sullivan Belinda didn't try.

She backed the car smartly out, barely missing a sapling that somehow sprang up in her path. And was it any wonder? Lucas had her so confused she could hardly breathe, let alone see.

What was he doing back there? Was he watching her leave? She didn't dare risk looking in her rearview mirror.

Lucas proposed. The thought whirled in her mind. By the time she reached her shop she was a nervous wreck. Thank goodness she had mountains of pies and cakes to bake. That ought to keep him off her mind for a while.

Chapter Seventeen

When Mandy got home that evening, two dozen roses waited for her, half red, half yellow.

"They came for you about an hour ago," Evelyn said. "I thought I'd die of curiosity before you got home. Hurry up and open the cards."

Mandy went to the vase of yellow roses first. She couldn't have said why, but they had always been her favorite. These were beauties, the buds cupped exactly right, unfurled just enough to see that when they opened fully the flowers would be spectacular.

She buried her nose in the bouquet and inhaled. "Lovely," she said.

"Open the card, Mandy."

Mandy enjoyed suspense, so she dallied over the card, tapping it against her hand, musing. "I'll bet Josie and Myrtle did all this."

"What in the world for?"

"Because I've had such a nasty, rotten day. Lucas proposed this morning…. Now, Mother, don't get excited. He didn't mean a word he said."

"How do you know?"

"I just do, that's all."

Mandy slid the card from the envelope. "Mandy," it read, "I meant every word I said. And I don't intend to take no for an answer. Lucas."

"Well?" Evelyn prompted. "Who sent them?"

"A certain stubborn Sioux we both know." Mandy jerked the vase up. "Mother, throw these in the garbage can, please."

"I will do no such thing."

"Then take them to your bedroom. I don't want to see them."

There had been absolutely no mention of love on Lucas's card. Even old Mr. Binky Blake signed *Love, Binky* on the card that came with his annual box of Valentine candy.

Mandy jerked up the vase of red roses, so mad she was shaking. "And take these with you."

"Aren't you going to open the card?"

"I know who sent them. *Lucas.*" He'd promised to lay siege to her fort. He was covering all bases.

"If you're not going to open the card, I am." Evelyn slid it from the envelope, then passed it to Mandy. "I think you should see this."

Mandy glanced at the signature first, then flabbergasted, she read the note: "Honey, I made a terrible mistake. I'm coming home to you and the kids. Chuck."

"This is unbelievable," she said. "What unmitigated gall."

"You'd think after all these years he'd at least know your favorite color." Evelyn said.

"I don't care what color they are." Mandy marched into the kitchen, poured the water down the drain, then heaved the flowers into the trash.

Evelyn followed her, setting the yellow roses on the table.

"How dare he think he can run off with the *love of his life,* then come crawling back to me."

Mandy was panting with effort. "Mother, if he shows his face on this property, shoot him," she said, then marched upstairs. She didn't care if it was only seven o'clock. She was going to say good-night to the children, then crawl into bed and forget about everybody except herself and her baby.

"You can ditch the visit to the lawyer," Lucas told Steve. He was in a phone booth somewhere near Franklin, Tennessee, his GoldWing parked nearby. "I've decided to marry her."

"When did you decide that?"

"This morning." He pictured how Mandy had looked sitting on the picnic bench with the sun in her hair and the lake behind her. Pregnancy had made her bloom, made her glow. But it wasn't just her pregnancy that had been the deciding point: it was *need.*

All of a sudden he'd known that he needed her, had needed her all along. That's why he had taken her into the woods. That's why he hadn't been able to get her out of his mind all summer. That's why he had turned his bike toward Mississippi instead of going to California.

It shocked Lucas to admit such a thing, even to himself. Need was for other people. Not for Lucas Gray Wolf. Need scared him nearly as much as love.

"Do you love her, Lucas?"

Did he? Is that what love was all about, knowing he couldn't live without her?

"I don't know, Lucas. All I know is that I have to have her."

Steve chuckled. "You're getting there, pal."

"What am I supposed to do now, Steve?"

"Send flowers."

"I already did."

"Send candy. Better yet, take it to her. Women love gifts. And, Lucas, take all the time you need. We're fine out here. Jenny Cordova and Britt Ace are coming next week. Said something about Angel helping to plan their wedding. Then Angel's dad and Kaki are coming for Thanksgiving."

"How's Angel?"

"You remember Flowergirl, that ornery pregnant filly we had last summer? Angel's got her beat by a country mile."

"I heard that." It was Angel, in the background. There was the sound of kissing, then she came on the phone. "Lucas, don't pay any mind to a thing Thunderhorse said. There's only one way to win your woman, and that's to tell her that you love her."

Lucas was so shaken he didn't know what he said to Angel. Did he love Mandy? If love tore a man into a million pieces, he didn't want any part of it. He made his hasty goodbyes, then turned his GoldWing south toward Saltillo.

He had a box of candy to buy and a woman to see.

Mandy couldn't believe her eyes when Chuck's old Ford pickup pulled into the driveway. The sound of the engine had brought her out of bed. She'd have known it anywhere.

He was getting bald. There was a spot on the top of his head as big as a silver dollar that reflected the moon. He had a paunch, too—not a big one, but enough extra flab so that it hung over his belt.

Mandy felt hot all over. Hot with outrage, hot with pregnancy, hot with a fever that she could only call *Lucas.* She flung open the window to cool herself off, then drew a straight-backed chair up and sat down to hide her condition.

Chuck was wearing so much cologne, she could smell him before he reached the front porch. Mandy didn't know why men dumped that stuff all over themselves. She'd always preferred the man's natural smell, especially an outdoorsman like Lucas.

Memories swamped her. Lucas smelled like sunshine and wind and earth. Last summer she'd spent a great deal of time with her face buried in his chest hair merely inhaling him.

Chuck was at the porch now, with one alligator-skin boot on the front steps.

"Don't take another step," Mandy said. He glanced up at the window, startled.

"Mandy..." He smoothed down his thinning hair, tucked his belly into his belt, then smiled so big the moon glinted on the gold fillings at the back of his mouth. "Lord, if you're not a sight for sore eyes."

"Where's the love of your life, Chuck? Playing Barbie dolls with her little friends?"

"I deserve that, hon. Lord knows, I do."

"Don't you *hon* me. Get off my property."

"Now, hon, don't be that way. A man can make a little mistake every now and then, can't he?"

"Divorcing me for another woman and ignoring your

children hardly qualifies as a *little mistake,* Chuck. It's more like an act of war.''

He wavered, uncertain. Mandy was proud of herself. When they'd been married, she'd rarely raised her voice to him. Somehow it had never seemed worth the effort.

''You're full of spit and vinegar, aren't you, gal? I kinda like that.'' He held up a big box wrapped in silver foil. ''I brought you some candy.''

''You know what you can do with that candy, Chuck.''

''Mandy?'' It was Evelyn, standing in the bedroom door in her nightgown. ''I heard voices. Is everything all right?''

''Go back to bed, Mother. There's just an old stray cur under my window. I'll take care of it.''

After Evelyn had gone, Mandy leaned out the window, taking care to hide her belly. ''See what you've done? You woke Mother. Don't you dare wake the children.''

''How are they? I want to see them.''

''I'll have my lawyer discuss it with your lawyer.'' Mandy jerked the curtains shut, then climbed into bed.

''Mandy?'' She wished she'd closed the window, but she was too tired to get up again and do it. ''Mandy? I'm not leaving.''

She heard the porch swing creak. He could sit out there all by himself till he turned into a pillar of salt for all she cared. Mandy pulled the quilt under her chin and tried to sleep.

There was somebody on Mandy's front porch. Lucas reached into his pack for his knife, then approached with stealth, though that was hardly called for since the GoldWing would have announced his presence a quarter of a mile back.

''Who's out there?''

It was a male voice. Lucas stopped in the shadow of the magnolia tree to study the intruder. Something silver glinted in his hand. A knife?

"What are you doing on Mandy's property?" Lucas called from the darkness.

"I'm Mandy's husband." Her *husband?* The fool who had left her? Or had she married somebody else while he was dithering around on his motorcycle? "Who are you?"

"Lucas Gray Wolf." He stepped into a path of moonlight. "The father of Mandy's baby."

Lucas strode onto the front porch. The man sitting in the swing was out of shape. Lucas could send him packing in a minute. And his present, too.

The man stood up, looking flustered...and five inches shorter than Lucas. At least.

"If you're talking about Jill, I'm her daddy. Betsy's and Rusty's too."

So, the man must be the infamous Chuck Belinda. Somehow, Lucas felt relieved. Mandy wouldn't give him the time of day.

Or would she? Lately, it was impossible to predict her.

"I'm not talking about Mandy's other three children. I'm talking about the baby she's going to have." Lucas sat on the porch swing, a move calculated to confuse Chuck Belinda. It worked. His mouth worked, but no words came out, and he squeezed his box so hard he crumpled it.

Candy, no doubt. Lucas was pleased to note that his box was bigger.

"Are you telling me Mandy's carrying a half-breed baby?"

"Sioux." He gave Mandy's ex-husband the famous Gray Wolf stare, the one that had sent better men than

Chuck Belinda skulking away. "I take scalps." He patted the knife in his belt.

Chuck scooted to the far end of the swing, but he didn't budge.

"You're lying." He propped his box on his knees and tried to smooth the paper. "I'm staying."

"So am I."

There was a commotion at the upstairs window, and Lucas looked up to see Mandy glaring down at them.

"What's this? The odd couple?"

"Mandy." Lucas stood up, determined to get an edge on his rival. "I brought you some chocolates." Lucas could have kicked himself. He sounded like a teenager.

"You wasted your money. Chocolate nauseates me."

"Mandy." Chuck Belinda stood beside Lucas like a sawed-off shadow. "Are you carrying this Indian's baby?"

Mandy vanished from the window so fast Lucas barely had time to register the look on her face. It boded ill for everybody.

"Where do you reckon she went?" Chuck said.

"I don't know, but if I were you, I'd hightail it out of here before she gets back."

Chuck dug his sissy boots into the porch and jutted out his jaw. He looked like an aging bulldog.

"I said I'm staying, and I meant what I said."

Stalemate. Lucas shifted his candy from one hand to the other. Hell would freeze over before he'd be the first to leave that front porch.

"You asked me a question, Chuck?" Mandy was back at the window, all sweetness and light. She didn't fool Lucas for a minute. There was pure hellfire and damnation behind her smile.

"Well, yeah, Mandy. I did."

"Here's your answer, Chuck." He was too slow to see what was coming.

Lucas sidestepped just as the water cascaded over Chuck. It was followed by wilted red roses with bits of cabbage leaves and orange peelings clinging to the stems.

Chuck sputtered and whacked at the garbage that had landed on the front of his shirt.

"Well, hell, Mandy..."

Lucas roared with laughter. It served the pompous old fool right, coming to court Mandy after dumping her.

"You think that's funny, Lucas?" Mandy hurled another bouquet out the window, vase and all. Her aim was deadly, but Lucas wasn't Sioux for nothing. The vase splintered harmlessly at his feet, yellow roses spilling across the porch.

"Now go home, both of you." Mandy slammed the window, then disappeared from view.

Chuck was already headed to his car. Lucas sat back down on the front porch swing. Mainly on principle. He wasn't about to let Chuck Belinda see him leave.

The taillights of his truck faded into the darkness, and Lucas stared at Mandy's bedroom window. Her spunk amazed him. Excited him. Invigorated him.

"I'm going to have to change your nickname from Lady to Wildcat," he said, then sat on the swing smiling into the darkness.

Chapter Eighteen

The phone woke Mandy up, which turned out to be a very good thing, for she'd slept through her alarm and was going to be late getting to the bakery.

Sitting on the edge of the bed she reached for her robe with one hand and the phone with the other.

"Hello."

"Mandy? It's me, Chuck."

"Goodbye…"

"Mandy, don't hang up. This is important."

"You have two minutes to say what's on your mind, Chuck."

"Listen, hon, I couldn't sleep last night for thinking about us."

"There is no *us*."

"I really do want to make it work for us again. Remember how it was?"

"*Bad* and *horrible* are two words that come to mind."

"I'll take that as a joke, Mandy."

"I'm not joking, Chuck. Goodbye."

"Mandy...wait. I...I've decided to forgive you if you'll take me back."

"Forgive me?"

"For that half-breed baby."

"Chuck, you know where you can go, and if I weren't such a lady, I'd tell you."

She hung up, and then said the word anyway. "Hell." It made her feel better. She raced through her bath, but even so she was still nearly an hour late. There was such a crowd outside her bakery she could hardly get in.

"What in the world's going on?"

She wasn't long finding out. As the crowd parted for her, she saw the first of the yellow roses. They filled her windows, taking every inch of space not occupied by baked goods. But it wasn't the roses that attracted all the attention—it was the cards and the man who'd sent them.

Every vase sported a white card with huge red letters that said, "Marry me, Mandy," and Lucas was standing in the doorway wearing a sandwich board painted with a bull's-eye.

When he spotted her, he came forward and caught her hands. "I wanted to give you something to aim at in case you said no."

The crowd cheered. "Say *yes*, Mandy," someone yelled, and the rest took up the chant. "Yes, yes, yes..."

"Never," she shouted, jerked her hands free and marched into her shop with all the dignity she could muster, which wasn't much considering that she was wearing her purple maternity top inside-out.

More flowers greeted her, yellow roses sprouting from every nook and cranny of the bakery. The fragrance nearly overwhelmed her.

"I'm going to be sick," she said.

Josie bustled from the kitchen, all smiles. "Isn't this the most romantic thing? I've never seen anything like it, Mandy, except maybe in the movies."

"That's what this is, Josie, a bad grade B movie, and that Sioux out there is nothing but an actor. Well, I have news for him. He doesn't fool me for a minute."

Josie's eyes got round and her mouth worked like a fish, but the only sound came from behind Mandy.

"This Sioux is not acting, Mandy."

She whirled on him. "Haven't you and Chuck done enough? Get out of my shop."

Lucas's face became a thundercloud. "What else has he done besides making a fool of himself last night?"

"He said he would forgive me for being pregnant."

"I'll scalp him."

If she hadn't known better, she'd have thought Lucas meant it. He was merely using a figure of speech, but Mandy had seen how much it had hurt him to hear his child referred to as a half-breed.

"I would help you, but I don't think it will cure his ignorance or his bad manners."

As if she weren't already turning to a pile of mush with Lucas standing in her shop surrounded by yellow roses, his smile further disarmed her.

Mandy put her hand on his arm. "Come with me, Lucas."

"Can I take the sandwich board off, or do you plan to use me for target practice?"

"Take it off. You're in no danger from me."

He was, of course, and had been from the minute he'd laid eyes on her. He propped his bull's-eye board in the corner between two enormous baskets of yellow roses, then followed her to a small cubicle barely big enough for the two of them.

And that was fine by Lucas. It gave him a chance to be close to her. A tiny line of sweat beaded her upper lip, and he longed to kiss it off.

But did he dare? He didn't know which direction to turn. He was already skating on thin ice with her.

She smiled at him, and he took that as a good sign.

"I really do love yellow roses, Lucas. How did you know they're my favorites?"

"I guess it would sound better if I said I'd inquired, but it was just a good guess, Mandy."

She sighed. "Not many people even bother to guess what I might like."

He imagined what her marriage to Chuck must have been like, the grinding routine, the lack of surprise, the loss of dreams. And now, here she was, once again pregnant and facing what must appear to her to be a bleak and joyless future.

Lucas wanted to give her all the things she longed for, but most of all, he wanted to give her back her dreams.

"Mandy..." He made a move to take her into his arms, but she held up her hand.

"No, Lucas. Please. I can't handle any more pressure."

"All right. No more pressure."

"No more proposals? Public or otherwise?"

In her present frame of mind, she would continue to say no.

"Agreed. No more proposals."

"Thank you, Lucas."

"I won't ask you to marry me again. I'll just wait around till you ask me."

For a minute, he thought she was going to throw something at him. Instead, she burst out laughing. Lucas was relieved.

"That's not going to happen, Lucas. Motorcycles aren't built for family travel, and over the years I've grown rather partial to living in a house, though if I had my druthers I'd live in something more up-to-date with lots of windows that would give me a panoramic view of the world."

She stood up, then arched and pressed her hands on her back. "You can go now, Lucas. I have work to do."

"I think I'll stick around."

"You'll be in the way. Besides, customers aren't allowed in the kitchen."

"I'm not a customer. I'm the new cook." With his hand on her elbow, he guided her in the direction of the kitchen, then nabbed an apron off the hook and tied it on. "Show me the dough, Mandy."

"You must be kidding. As if you didn't make a big enough mess in here already...."

He stopped her with a kiss. Just a small one. Just enough to taste. Then he led her to a chair.

"Sit and direct."

"You're crazy," she said, but she was laughing.

"Didn't I tell you, Lady? I got sent to the kitchen so many times at the orphanage I figured I might as well learn how to cook while I was repenting my evil ways."

He grabbed a large mixing bowl and set it on the cooking island. "What do you want me to do first, cakes or pies?"

Chapter Nineteen

"Mother, you didn't tell me you were going out."

Evelyn was in her best red silk dress, the one she saved for special occasions.

"I have a social life, too, you know."

"I'm sorry. I didn't mean it that way." Mandy checked on her children playing in the backyard, then poured herself a tall glass of milk, sat down and propped her feet up.

"Hard day?"

"Actually, no. I had extra help today." Mandy smiled, thinking of Lucas mixing cake batter. He'd amazed her with his proficiency. "Lucas."

"You don't say."

"You don't seem too surprised. Now why should that worry me?"

"Are you accusing me of consorting behind your back, Mandy?"

"I'm not accusing you, Mother. I'm just wondering why all of a sudden you're going somewhere dressed fit to kill, and I didn't even know the plans."

"You have enough on your mind without worrying about me and my doings." Evelyn checked her wristwatch. "Dear me, if I don't hurry I'm going to be late. Don't wait up for me."

It was only five-thirty. Too early for dinner. And she was overdressed for a game of bridge with her friends. And why in the world was she planning to stay out so late?

Could her mother have a boyfriend? Flabbergasted, Mandy stared at the door. Evelyn's perfume still lingered in the air.

The back screen door popped, and Rusty stomped into the room.

"Do you want some milk and cookies, Rusty?"

"Naw. Milk's for babies. I ain't drinking that sissy stuff no more."

"*I'm not* drinking it *any*more, Rusty, and of course you are."

"I'm the man of the house now. I'm gonna drink cola."

"The milk issue is not negotiable, and who told you that you were the man of the house?"

"I figured it out. See, Jimmy's mom's gonna have a baby, too, and Jimmy told me there's no such thing as having a baby without a man of the house."

Mandy's heart sank. If it weren't for her children, she wouldn't care what people said about her. And truth to tell, after the initial shock of her pregnancy had worn off, the adults in Saltillo had been supportive and kind. Often, it was the children you had to watch out for.

"I socked him in the belly and told him *I* was the man of the house."

"Oh, Rusty." Mandy gathered her oldest child in her arms. "You're just a little boy. You don't have to assume those grown-up responsibilities."

"I don't?"

"No. I'm the adult here. *I'll* be the man of the house."

He giggled as she'd hoped he would. "Can I have my milk and cookies outside?"

"You can. Betsy and Jill, too. I'll bring a tray outside and we'll have a picnic."

He raced across the kitchen, then skidded to a stop at the door, his cowlick bobbing. "Will you tell my sisters I'm too old to play dolls?"

"Yes, I will."

"Good, 'cause I quit today."

She stood at the door watching as her three children joined hands, then circled the yard, laughing. She treasured such moments.

As she fixed the tray for the backyard picnic, she pictured Lucas in a too-small apron snitching a bit of chocolate frosting when he thought no one was looking. Just like a little boy. He'd made twice as much banana cream frosting as he'd needed and sworn it wasn't deliberate. Then he'd handed out spoons and everybody gathered around the mixing bowl to eat leftover frosting, even Myrtle.

Dear Lord, was she making a mistake turning him down? Rusty had looked so small, recounting his man-of-the-house story. Her children adored Lucas, and he seemed genuinely fond of them. He would be a good father. That much Mandy knew. And he seemed determined to be a part of his baby's life.

Mandy sighed. Call her a romantic fool, but she refused to marry a man who didn't love her. No matter how much her heart was breaking.

Evelyn stopped at a service station and changed into her jeans. There was no way she could have left the house in jeans without arousing Mandy's suspicions.

She backed against the far wall and inspected herself in the tiny fly-specked mirror. "Not bad for an old girl," she said. Then she got into her car and drove to Lake Lamar Bruce.

"Mrs. Sullivan, thank you for agreeing to see me. I'm sorry you had to drive all the way out here, but it seemed the only way."

"Evelyn, please." She made herself comfortable on the picnic bench. "I thought we settled all that last summer." She patted a spot beside her on the bench. "Sit down, Lucas. And quit looking so uncomfortable. I'm on your side."

"I can't tell you what a relief that is. Right now, I need all the troops I can get."

Evelyn laughed. "You make this sound like a battle."

"It is. A battle of wills."

"You needn't tell me how stubborn that daughter of mine is. I already know. And I'll tell you the same as I told her—that I think she's wrong. She ought to say *yes* to your proposal so everybody can get on with their lives."

"I don't mean to disrupt your life, but I *do* intend to be a father to my baby. No matter what it takes."

"Good for you. I'm rooting for you all the way."

Evelyn patted his hand, and Lucas caught a glimpse of what it would be like to have a family of his own. The warmth, the closeness, the trust. Why had he ever thought it would be so hard?

"You're a good man, Lucas Gray Wolf. And I'll be proud to call you son-in-law. If that day ever comes."

"It's coming all right. I promise you that." Lucas shifted so he could look west toward the setting sun, west toward Paradise Ranch. He longed to be there, but the funny thing was, he didn't long to be there alone. Not anymore.

"It seems to me that Mandy missed out on a lot of things, marrying so young. I'd like to make up for that loss, give her back a few dreams. That's where you come in, Evelyn. I need you to tell me about Mandy."

"Oh, my, you are a romantic soul, aren't you?" Evelyn paused to wipe her eyes and blow her nose. "I'll do everything I can to help you. Where do you want me to start?"

"At the beginning."

Evelyn did, and a complete picture of her daughter emerged: Mandy was romantic to the bone with the simple dreams to match. He would have no trouble at all being Gray Wolf, the dream maker.

After Evelyn had finished talking, Lucas kissed her on the cheek. "Thank you," he said.

"Oh, my. If Mandy won't marry you, I will, myself."

Lucas laughed. "I see you wore your jeans. Does that mean you're ready to try the motorcycle?"

"Why not? I figured if I'm going to have a son-in-law who rides one of those things, I can't afford to be a prissy wimp. Where's that helmet you said you had?"

Lucas fitted Evelyn's stiff, poufed hair into the helmet, and she laughed about needing a new style. When they were both on the GoldWing he said, "Hang on, Evelyn. You're not scared, are you?"

"I'm giddy is all. This is going to be the ride of my life." She clutched his shoulders. "Let 'er rip."

* * *

Mandy was in the kitchen making coffee when Evelyn came downstairs.

"You were out awfully late last night, Mother. I waited up till eleven o'clock."

"I told you not to wait up."

It was maddening the way Evelyn poured herself a cup of coffee, then became immersed in the paper.

"You never read the paper before the children and I leave. What's up?"

"You have a suspicious turn of mind, Mandy." Evelyn flipped to the society section. "Gertrude Willis's daughter is getting married. And here's Beaulah Grady's girl. Never thought I'd see the day she'd land a man."

"Mother, it won't work."

"What won't work?"

"All those not-so-subtle reminders of my husbandless state."

"For goodness sake, Mandy. I'm not talking about you. I'm discussing the neighbors." She patted the satin cap she'd slept in to keep her hair in place. "I'm thinking about a new hairdo. What do you think?"

"Great. Get something that doesn't inflict the torture of perms and curlers."

As Mandy was pouring her coffee, the phone rang. Though the phone was not two feet away from Evelyn, she kept reading her paper.

"Mother, aren't you going to get that?"

"Why don't you, dear? I'm busy."

If she'd seen the way Evelyn was smiling as she disappeared behind the society section, Mandy might not have answered. As it was, she was totally unprepared for Lucas Gray Wolf.

"Good morning, Mandy," he said, as if he were in the habit of calling her every day. "How are you today?"

"Pregnant."

Lucas roared with laughter.

"I don't see what's so funny about that. You should try getting into pantyhose when you can't see your feet."

"Need any help?"

"Not from you."

"I'd be good at it."

"How do you know?"

"I'm good at everything."

"You're in a jovial mood. Now, why does that scare me?"

"Relax, Lady. No more front porch scenes. At least not for a while. By the way, is that fool Chuck still in town?"

"No. He called this morning to say he'd changed his mind again and was going back to try and patch things up with little Miss Muffet. He wished me luck."

Lucas was quiet for so long, Mandy thought she'd lost the connection. "Lucas, are you still there?"

"I'm here. I'm sorry you had to go through that, Mandy."

Heavy with pregnancy and tears, Mandy sat down. Nothing touched her emotions quicker than sincere sympathy.

"Sometimes I think you're a good man, Lucas Gray Wolf."

"Hold that thought till I get back."

She couldn't believe her ears. "You're leaving?"

"Yes. For a little while." Wasn't that exactly what she wanted? Wasn't that what she'd been telling him to do? "Don't worry, Mandy, I'll be back."

Why should he? She'd been nothing but a shrew since

he came, and she was big as a barrel besides. On the other hand, he hadn't been any picnic himself.

"Don't bother," she snapped.

"If you're going to take that attitude, you won't be any fun at all on the honeymoon."

He hung up before she could think of a tart reply. His news shook her more than she cared to admit, and she turned her frustration on her mother.

"Isn't that just like a man? Disappear at the first sign of trouble." Mandy jerked up her cup and took a drink of cold coffee. "I, for one, am through. Do you hear me? I wouldn't touch Lucas Gray Wolf with a ten-foot pole."

Chapter Twenty

The gathering of friends took place at sunset on Paradise Ranch. For the past hour, Angel and Steve had sat on the sofa holding hands while Lucas told them how he planned to be dream maker to Mandy Sullivan Belinda.

Lucas was nervous in the telling. He'd left some things out—the intimate details, naturally—and some other things too deeply personal to share even with good friends. He knew he hadn't told his story well, and yet when he finished, Angel had tears in her eyes.

"That's so beautiful," she said. "Almost as beautiful as the love story between Steve and me."

"This is not a love story," Lucas said quickly, too quickly, he guessed, because Steve and Angel both smiled at him in the way of indulgent parents who know when a child is being too stubborn to tell the truth.

"It's more of a…a plan for the future of my child."

"You haven't told her you love her?" Angel said.

Naturally, she would take the romantic viewpoint. That was a female trait. Lucas looked to his friend Steve for support.

"You won't get any help from me on that one, pal." Steve chuckled.

"Surely Mandy will see the logic of my plan."

Angel snorted. "Talk some sense into him, Steve. I'm going to eat ice cream."

"Again, darling?" Three empty bowls sat on the coffee table bearing telltale evidence of butterscotch ice cream with chocolate topping.

Angel gave him an aggrieved look, then left the room, supporting her big belly with her hands.

It was Lucas's turn to laugh. "Looks like you're in the doghouse."

"That's where I usually am, lately." Steve jumped up to follow his wife. "Take my advice, pal. Don't ever forget you're dealing with a pregnant woman. If you hope to win the battle with her, you'd better plan a perfect campaign."

He paused in the doorway. "By the way, Gray Wolf, I know the courage it took to face your ghosts. I'm proud to be your friend."

Steve hurried to his wife's side while Lucas unfolded a sketch he'd taken from his pocket and spread it on the table. It was his vision for a house. Mandy's vision, really. She wanted lots of windows, she'd said, the feeling of being outdoors even when she was inside.

Lucas knew he could never achieve that. He knew he could never capture the feel of wind against his face, the pungent smell of the earth beneath his back.

His pulse quickened at the thought of living within four walls. Thunderhorse had lauded his bravery in facing the past and putting old ghosts to rest.

But had he? Lucas folded the sketch and put it back in his pocket. Only time would tell.

The leaves turned gold, then fell from the trees in heaps that scrunched under Mandy's feet. Fall had come to Mississippi late, as usual. Mandy swapped short sleeves for sweaters. And where was Lucas?

She kicked a pile of leaves, then held her belly in quick remorse as her baby protested with jabs worthy of a prizefighter. Thanksgiving would be here before Mandy knew it, then Christmas and the new year. And then she would have her baby. Alone.

But not scared. By George, she refused to be scared.

Chin high, she turned the corner at Elm Street and headed back to her house, puffing. She'd never been this big with the others.

Mr. Binky Blake was in his yard raking leaves. "Hello, Mandy." He leaned his rake against the fence and tipped his hat. "You're looking beautiful today, as usual."

"Thank you. It must be all this fresh air."

"No. It's just you. I've always said you're the prettiest little thing in Saltillo." His confession made him blush.

"Why, thank you, Mr. Blake. You're very sweet."

In fact, all her friends were being exceptionally thoughtful. Including Josie and Myrtle. When she got to her shop, she called them both into her office for a conference.

"First I want to thank both of you for carrying more than your share of the workload around here. Maybe it's my age, but this pregnancy is different from the others. I don't know how much longer I'll be able to work."

"Don't you worry about a thing," Josie said. "Myrtle and I can run this bakery." Myrtle nodded vigorously.

"Great. I'm putting the two of you in charge of the

kitchen, and Millicent Jones will be joining our staff Saturday.''

"Humph," Myrtle sniffed. ''I'll have to teach her to make piecrusts. Hers are stiff as boards.''

"She'll be doing the business end of the bakery.''

"If she's bossing, it'll go to her head,'' Myrtle added.

"Now, Myrtle, she's a good woman,'' Josie said, and Mandy knew she'd chosen wisely.

"When I'm not here, Josie's in charge.''

They were both beaming as Mandy hurried off to her appointment with her doctor.

"There's no question, Mandy,'' he said. ''You're going to have twins.''

Sitting on the sofa watching a late-night rerun of *Gone with the Wind,* Mandy told her mother what the doctor had said. Both of them were crying over Rhett's gift of a frivolous hat to Scarlett, and when Mandy told her about the twins they cried even harder.

"I suspected it all along, but I didn't say anything,'' Evelyn said. ''Pity you didn't have that sonogram last summer. Then you could have told Lucas.''

"What difference would it have made?''

"Don't you worry.'' Evelyn reached for Mandy's hand, then held on. ''We'll get through this just fine.''

Oh, Lord, Mandy was thinking. *Three, and soon five.*

"You bet we will,'' she told her mother. ''This is fabulous news.''

They cried all the way through Scarlett's honeymoon, through the deaths of Bonnie Blue and Melanie, and by the time Rhett uttered his famous disclaimer, they could barely see through their tears.

"See what happens when you're stubborn?'' Evelyn said. ''You lose the love of your life.''

"Who? Chuck? He and Shirley Temple are on a second honeymoon cruise on the Good Ship Lollipop."

Evelyn swatted Mandy with the TV listings while she turned off the set with the remote control. They sat in the dark for a while letting Margaret Mitchell's sweeping saga of love and war settle into them. Then Mandy stood up, stretching.

"I'm going to bed. Good night, Mother."

"Night." She caught her daughter's hand as she walked past. "Don't you worry about a thing. Lucas will be back."

Mandy bit back her quick protest. Whether it was the darkness or the camaraderie of watching a classic movie they both loved, or the news that she would give birth to two, Mandy didn't know, but something about the moment demanded truth.

"I hope so, Mother. I *do* hope so."

Lucas's letter arrived in the mail the next day, a large, brown envelope that Mandy tucked into her handbag and carried upstairs to the bedside table. Jill and Betsy were waiting in the kitchen for cookies and milk; Rusty was telling about his latest school project that involved an aviator named Jim Standing Bear, and Evelyn poked her head through the door and asked if Mandy had any laundry.

The letter would have to wait.

In order to get to the house site he had chosen, Lucas, along with his architect and his contractor, rode horses. A road would have to be built.

"Start tomorrow," Lucas said. Everybody agreed that was no problem. "I want to be in the house by Christmas," he told them, and they said, "Impossible."

"March, then. The baby's coming in March."

"Can't promise, but we'll try."

Lucas crossed *house* off his mental list, then headed into town for the last of his errands.

When she was finally alone in her bedroom, Mandy slit open the manila envelope, and out tumbled the house plans. A yellow sticky note was attached. "For us, Mandy." No signature, just a stamp with the sign of the wolf.

The house was her dream come true—a sprawling, modern affair with plenty of wide, sweeping windows and more skylights than she'd imagined a house could have. The rooms were spacious, each one with a view. Lucas had not only planned separate bedrooms for each of the children, but a grand suite for Evelyn, too.

Mandy traced each line of the house, imagining how each room would look, the colors she would use, the exact placement of furniture, even the artwork on the walls. She stared at the house until the lines blurred, then she searched the manila envelope for a note. There was none.

She turned the plans over to see if he'd written anything on the back—the location of the house, a personal note, a signature. Anything, anything at all.

There was nothing. Not even the date.

"Oh, Lucas." Why couldn't he have at least signed the yellow sticky note? Why couldn't he have at least written "fondly"?

She folded the plans, slid them back into the envelope, then slid the whole thing under her pillow. A girl could still dream, couldn't she?

Two days later, another envelope from Arizona arrived, this one containing a color brochure of Venice, and two tickets to Italy. The note was blue this time. "Pack your bags. We're going on a honeymoon."

He'd scrawled his name, but no endearments, not even "Yours truly."

Mandy put his latest communication under her pillow with the house plans. Soon her pillow was going to be too elevated for her to sleep, let alone dream.

When she went to bed that evening she dreamed that she was in a gondola with Lucas. The moon was shining, music was playing, and he was saying, "I love you, Mandy."

And somewhere in the middle of Texas, Lucas Gray Wolf was making his way to Mississippi—without his GoldWing.

Chapter Twenty-One

Mandy had slept like a log in spite of the huge lump under her pillow. She showered, then went downstairs to make coffee, but her mother was already there, hanging up the telephone.

"Mother, who was that on the phone?"

"What phone?" Mandy put her hands on her hips, but Evelyn merely looked smug. "Oh, that? Nobody, dear. Drink your coffee."

"I don't drink coffee now, remember?" Mandy started rummaging in the cabinet for cereal, but Evelyn took the box right out of her hand.

"I thought I'd make pecan waffles this morning."

"Fine, Mother, whatever you like, but I have to get to the bakery."

"Good grief, Mandy, it's Saturday. Why don't you wait a while and have waffles with us?"

"Because Saturday is my busiest day." She took the

box back and poured herself a bowl of cereal, then went to the refrigerator for her milk. When she came back, her bowl had vanished. So had the cereal box.

"Mother, what is this? I don't have time for these games."

"This is not a game. I can have the waffles made by the time you're dressed."

Mandy didn't have enough energy to argue. As she started up the stairs her mother called after her, "Mandy, wear something pretty. That green top. It brings out your eyes."

She'd been thinking about the green top anyhow since Millicent was coming in after lunch and Mandy wanted to look as professional as possible, but her stubborn streak made her grab her old brown one out of the closest.

She was in front of the mirror thinking how much she resembled a stuffed sausage when the commotion in the yard drew her to the window. There was a brand-new van parked under the trees and behind it was a huge trailer with tails sticking out all around.

"What fresh hell is this?" Mandy muttered. Lately she'd embraced Dorothy Parker wholeheartedly.

Mandy hurried to the head of the stairs and called down to Evelyn. "Mother, if that's somebody selling something, tell them we don't want any."

"You might want to tell him yourself, dear. My hands are in the pecan waffle batter."

Mandy sighed and started down. The staircase looked ten miles long.

"I'll do it, Mama." Rusty bounced past her, then burst open the door and gave a rebel yell. "It's Lucas!"

Mandy thought she'd die on the spot. She could see him through the door Rusty had left standing open, tall and bronzed and totally gorgeous, and here she was not only looking her fattest, but wearing the ugliest thing in her closet.

She hurried as fast as she could back up the stairs. No sooner was her door shut than clothes and shoes went flying. He couldn't see her in jogging shoes, for goodness sakes. She grunted as she bent down to put on her good black pumps, then grabbed the brush on the way to her closet for her green top.

Mandy paused with the brush in midair. Lucas's laughter was rich and full-bodied, his voice deep and deliciously sexy. She had to see him.

She dashed to the window and there he was, standing in the sunshine with her children hanging onto him as if they'd won him in the toss-the-ring-on-the-bottle booth at the country fair.

Her heart stood still. It was that sentimental, that simple. Standing beneath her window was the man she loved beyond all reason, and for a moment time, and even life itself, stood in silent, awesome suspension.

Mandy covered the two little heartbeats with her hands and gazed down at him. He was driving a van. He'd sent house plans. He'd sent honeymoon brochures.

At long last, Lucas Gray Wolf had come to tell her that he loved her.

Something alerted him, a sound at the window, the sense of someone watching, the magnetic pull of a heart too full to speak.

He looked up and saw her. And smiled. Such a smile. She'd never seen a thing so beautiful. Never taking her eyes off his, Mandy opened the window.

"Hello, Lucas," she said.

He let his eyes answer first. They roamed over her with a hunger that took her breath away.

"Hello, Lady. You look beautiful. The green matches your eyes."

Mandy sighed. She was going to burn that ugly brown top. From now on, every piece of clothing she bought was going to be green.

She told him thank you. He'd called her Lady; she called him Lucas. And then she'd simply stood still, overwhelmed with tenderness.

Lucas thought he'd prepared himself for his first glimpse of Mandy, but he hadn't. How was it that a grown man could stand speechless underneath the window of a woman in green? How was it that everything he'd so carefully planned to say flew straight out of his mind?

The sun in her hair had always mesmerized him. Maybe that was it. Or perhaps it was the Madonna-like quality she exuded as she stood with her hands cupped protectively around her belly.

With the lace curtains billowing around her, she was a vision that filled his soul, a dream that awakened his heart. Need clamored through him, and "love" was on the tip of his tongue, but he dared not speak it.

Everything he'd ever loved had been taken from him, swept away in blazes so hot the scars were seared into his soul. He would keep love to himself. He would name it need, and hope that he'd fooled fate. He would call it the future and pray the powers that be would never find out the true nature of his feelings.

"Where's your GoldWing bike?" she said.

"Back home in Arizona. This is my new chariot. Do you like it?"

"Yes. It's big."

"Big enough for a family, I hope."

He loved the way her smile turned to laughter, loved the way she tipped back her head so that the sun shimmered on her lovely white throat. He longed to touch her, couldn't wait to touch her.

"Come on down, Mandy, and see what else I brought."

"Hurry, Mama," Rusty yelled.

Beside him, the children were jumping up and down with excitement. He'd sworn them to secrecy the minute they'd come out the front door.

Mandy vanished from the window, and Lucas had to restrain himself from racing up to the stairs to meet her. He would play it cool. That's what he'd decided to do on the long drive from his house to hers.

Flushed and breathless, she appeared at the door, and all his plans went up in smoke. He raced up the stairs, scooped her into his arms and whirled around the front porch.

"Good grief, Lucas," she protested, but she was laughing. "What in the world are you doing?"

"Dancing with my girl."

"My feet are supposed to be on the ground."

"Are you saying I've swept you off your feet?"

She glanced toward her children, then whispered, "Something like that."

He wanted to kiss her. Standing right there on the front porch in view of her children, the neighbors, and God. But he knew that once he started he would have a hard time stopping.

Instead, he carried her down the front steps and deposited her among her children.

"Guess what's in the trailer, Mandy?"

"I'll give you a hint, Mama," Rusty said. "They have tails."

"I can see that."

Jill was jumping up and down in her excitement. "It's a secret, Mommy. It's not horses."

"Jill *told*," Betsy said. "You weren't supposed to *tell*, Jill."

Jill teared up, and Lucas squatted down to hug her. "It's all right, kitten. See those tails sticking out of the trailer? Mommy had already guessed."

"Horses, Lucas? You brought your *horses?*"

"Not my horses, Mandy. Yours."

"Mine?"

"Yes, it's the Sioux way." He lowered the tailgate and led three gentle paints into the yard—horses he'd trained specifically for kids. "These are gifts for the children."

Their squeals brought Evelyn running, and the children all started talking at once, bringing her up-to-date and trying to decide which horse they wanted.

In the midst of the hubbub, Lucas tethered the horses and then moved to stand close to Mandy. She smelled like spring flowers.

"What do you think, Mandy?"

"You leave me speechless."

"Good." He smiled down at her. "If we didn't have such a large audience, I'd kiss you."

"What am I going to do with three horses, pray tell?"

"I've arranged for the Grayton Stables outside Saltillo to board them."

"Lucas, I can't..."

He touched her lips with the tips of his fingers. "Shh. I've taken care of everything." Her lips were soft and moist, irresistible. He traced them with his fingertips.

"You don't play fair," she whispered.

"I warned you I was going to lay siege to your fort, Lady."

"Is this about the baby?"

Her eyes held his, and there was something in their depths he couldn't quite figure out.

"It's about us."

"Us, Lucas?"

"Yes, us. You know, the house, the van big enough for all of us, the honeymoon in Venice."

"How did you know I've always wanted to go to Venice?"

"I inquired."

He laced his fingers through hers and held on while he watched the play of sunlight in her eyes. At that moment, he knew with absolute certainty that the last thing he wanted to see before he departed this earth was those emerald eyes shining down from Mandy's dear face.

Almost, he told her he loved her. *Almost.*

How the fates would laugh. *Gotcha!* they'd say. Lucas drew a deep breath and waited until the moment passed.

A telltale hint of moisture shimmered in Mandy's eyes. "Are you asking me to marry you?" she whispered.

"I'm waiting for you to ask me, remember?"

"I remember."

She was watching him again with that waiting stillness that he found disconcerting. He held her gaze so long that she literally stole his breath. Then he turned her hand over and kissed the soft palm.

"There's something I have to tell you, Lucas. I guess this is as good a time as any."

The children were still clamoring over the horses and, the best Lucas could tell, Evelyn was now acting as referee, mediator and judge.

"I'm going to have twins," Mandy said.

Lucas felt gut-punched, and whether it was from pride or shock, he couldn't say. The yard was full of people.

Mandy had three children and two on the way. Add Evelyn, then the two of them.

One passionate moment in June and Lucas had gone from being a lone wolf to the head of a household of eight.

Mandy took umbrage at his silence. She jerked her hand out of his.

"You're under no obligation, whatsoever. You never have been and you never will be." She stalked off, then turned her head to say over her shoulder, "Get out of my yard, Lucas Gray Wolf...and take your horses with you."

"Mandy, wait." She didn't, of course. Stubborn redhead that she was. And pregnant, to boot. What had he expected?

She stomped up the front steps and slammed into the house. Lucas followed her.

"I'll keep the children out here," Evelyn yelled after him, as if they would possibly want to go anywhere else.

"The horses are gentle, but don't let them try to ride until I get back."

Mandy was already halfway up the stairs. She'd be in her bedroom soon with the door locked against him. He'd hate to break it down. As a matter of fact, he didn't know whether or not he could. It wasn't one of the cheap doors some people put in modern houses, but a substantial door carved of solid oak, built to last, just the way the house had been constructed—to bear up through several generations of family.

"Mandy, wait..." He took the stairs two at a time, but she put on a burst of speed and was already in her bedroom before he'd gained the landing.

"I'm happy about the babies, Mandy. Really, I am."

She slammed the door, and the lock clicked into place.

Lucas stood on the other side and tapped. "Mandy? Let me in. We need to talk."

"You've said all I want to hear. Go back to Arizona, Lucas.... Better yet, go out to California and get yourself a golden girl."

"A Valley girl."

"I don't care if she's a tree dweller. Just go away."

He tapped again. "Mandy...please open the door."

Silence. He hadn't heard footsteps. Mandy was just on the other side of the door, listening.

Good. At least she was curious.

Using the stealth of his ancestors, Lucas stole down the stairs and out the front door.

But he wasn't headed to California. Not by a long shot.

Chapter Twenty-Two

Mandy had always prided herself on being a reasonable woman, and yet here she was locked in her bedroom to get away from Lucas. She felt silly and foolish, and her feet hurt, besides.

She kicked off the pumps, then stretched out on her bed to take the weight off her feet. She was very close to tears. Was love too much to ask of a man who was practically offering the moon?

Outside her window, she could hear the excited chatter of her children. Lucas would make a good father for them. Was she being selfish denying them that?

A breeze stirred and magnolia branches scratched against her window. Mandy closed her eyes. Maybe she'd get lucky and fall asleep, and when she woke up everything would be back to normal.

What *was* normal, anyhow? All her life it seemed she'd been hanging onto the edge of abnormal, marrying

Chuck because she had to, having her children so fast she'd never had time to think about anything except raising a family.

Fortunately she was good at it. Lucky for them all she'd have chosen exactly that kind of life for herself, being a mother and taking care of other people. But, oh, it would be so lovely if somebody would take care of her right back. Somebody who loved her.

The curtains rustled, and Mandy was glad she'd left the window open. She did love to sleep with a good breeze blowing through the room. A little catnap was exactly what she needed. Afterwards, she'd go to the bakery and introduce Millicent to the business end of Lucky Mandy's.

"Mandy."

Her eyes snapped open. Lucas was standing beside her bed looking like someone who'd stepped out of her dreams.

"Good grief. How did you get in?"

"Through the window."

"You climbed a tree to get into my bedroom?"

He knelt beside her bed and held her hand. "Lady, I'd climb a mountain to get into your bedroom." His thumbs massaged her palms. "I'd swim a river, brave the desert…"

"Enough." How could she help but laugh at him? "If you overdo it, I won't believe you."

"Believe me, Mandy. Believe *in* me."

Lucas was a dangerous man to have in the bedroom. The intimacy of the setting enhanced his intensity, his persuasiveness. He seduced her with his eyes, with his hands.

They moved upward to her wrists. Bending over, he planted hot kisses where her blue veins crisscrossed, then he made small erotic circles with his thumbs. She sucked in a trembling breath.

"I'm going to close my eyes and pretend this is a dream," she whispered, and then she did.

"I dream of you, Mandy." He slid his hands upward, then began to massage the inside of her elbows. "Do you dream of me?"

"Yes." She licked her dry lips. "Sometimes." *Often. Always. Every night.*

He traced her lips with his forefinger, then let it slide slowly into her mouth. She had to taste him. Any sane woman would. As her lips closed around his finger, she kept her eyes closed, hoping he wouldn't see what he was doing to her.

"Hmm, good," he murmured.

She felt the mattress sag, felt his hip pressed against hers, felt the shock as his right hand slid under her maternity top and came to rest on her distended belly.

"I'm fat," she said.

"You're beautiful."

She wanted to believe him. She didn't dare open her eyes for fear of seeing a lie.

His finger kept doing deliciously wicked things on the inside of her mouth.

"I feel the babies...I *feel* the babies."

Mandy's eyes snapped open. The wonder she'd heard in his voice was reflected in his face. She'd never loved another as much as she loved Lucas at that moment.

"Oh, Lucas." She opened her arms, and he came to her, lay down beside her, and kissed her with such tenderness that she cried. He kissed her tears away, then took her mouth once more. It was exquisite, breathtaking, redemptive.

"Thank you for the horses..." she whispered.

"You're more than welcome. I'll teach the children how to ride."

"...and the van..."

"I hope we all fit."

"...and the house. Oh, Lucas, thank you most of all for the house."

He unbuttoned her top, then folded it back and gazed down at her. And for the first time ever, Mandy felt beautiful in her pregnancy. She felt lush and ripe and content and sexy. *Yes,* she even felt sexy.

Lucas confirmed everything she was feeling with his eyes, his hands, his mouth. Her nipples responded instantly to his touch, and when he took them in his mouth, she laced her fingers through his hair and held him close.

For the moment, she was content. Call me decadent, she thought. Call me selfish. Call me bad to the bone.

Luca was here, the door was locked, and the children were outside. She *needed* him. After months of carrying the burden of her pregnancy alone, after years of being the backbone of her family, she needed the affirmation of physical intimacy. She needed to feel desirable. She needed to feel *needed.*

And only one man could do that. Lucas Gray Wolf, the incredible Sioux who suckled so tenderly at her breasts.

He lifted his head to look at her and his eyes flamed like bright blue blazes. "I'm not hurting you, am I?"

"No," she whispered, drawing him down to her once more. "Never."

They shifted in the bed to make more room for Lucas, and both babies kicked so hard he jerked back, astonished.

"Did they do that?"

"Yes."

He put his face against her stomach and rubbed his cheek gently across her pale skin. "My babies," he murmured. "My babies." Then he covered her abdomen with kisses.

She felt cherished. Her love for him overflowed, and she gave it voice.

"I love you, Lucas," she whispered. He went still, and she held her breath, waiting. Her heart thumped so hard against her chest she could almost hear its pounding.

Suddenly, everything around her was magnified: the ticking of the bedside clock, the distant echo of her children's laughter, the sound of Lucas's breathing. She saw his eyes in sharp detail, the blue so deep it spilled into the white, shading it almost the color of a robin's egg. She saw a tiny star-shaped scar on his chin she'd never noticed.

Say it, she silently pleaded. *Say I love you right back.*

A trickle of sweat worked its way from underneath his hair and ran down his cheek. Still, he was silent.

She saw struggle in his face, longing, pain, such pain that she could no longer bear to look. She closed her eyes, suddenly weary.

She was big and cumbersome and much too tired to fight. As much as it hurt her pride to admit it, she needed Lucas. Evelyn would have her hands full with Rusty and Jill and Betsy. It was unfair of Mandy to expect her to help take care of two more babies.

"You win, Lucas." She opened her eyes. He was still staring down at her with such an agony of longing and fear that she wrapped her arms around herself, shivering. "I'm not going to fight you anymore."

"We'll have a quiet wedding," he said. "Just family and good friends."

Anger gave her enough energy to jerk her maternity

top shut. "Make no mistake, Lucas Gray Wolf. I am *not* asking you to marry me. As a matter of fact, I wouldn't touch a wedding certificate with a ten-foot pole."

"But you said you'd changed your mind."

"I have, but not about the marriage. I said I won't *fight* anymore. You can hang around till the babies are born. My mother could use some help and so can I."

He simply shut down. That was the only way to describe how he looked, eyes hooded, face shuttered. She couldn't have read what he was thinking if she'd been a fortune teller.

"I'm going to stick around, all right. Permanently."

"You'll do no such thing."

"I thought you weren't going to fight anymore."

Mandy started to protest, but she'd run out of steam. "You're right. Fighting solves nothing."

The buttons on her maternity top refused to cooperate. She was still fumbling around, half-exposed. And Lucas made no bones about the fact that he was looking.

"You can have the bedroom down the hall," she said.

"Fine." He pushed her hands aside.

"What are you doing?"

"You asked for my help. I'm giving it to you."

He was fastening her buttons, of course, but ever so much more. His hands were all over her, massaging and caressing her skin, lifting and molding her breasts, subtly circling her nipples.

She wondered how long she was going to be able to hold out with Lucas Gray Wolf just down the hall. And her as big as a fattening hog.

Her libido had cooperated beautifully when she was carrying her other children. For a few weeks, she and Chuck had gone through the motions, but it never seemed worth the effort. Both of them had been glad when she finally suggested that it might be best if they refrained.

Lucas Gray Wolf was another story. She was on fire all over. Even as big as she was she'd stand on the bed and do a striptease if he'd only say the right words.

They didn't even have to be *I love you.* At this stage of the game she'd settle for something more modest, something along the line of *I care for you.*

Lucas finished putting her clothes back in order, and was sitting on her bed looking at her in a way that did nothing to put out her fires. Why didn't he say something?

The buzz of excitement was still going on underneath the window. Her children and her mother, filled with great expectations.

"You can stay for breakfast," Mandy said. "Mother is making pecan waffles."

And now she knew why. Of course Evelyn had known about Lucas's coming. What else did she know?

"That's very kind of you." He stood up. "Afterward I'll move my things into the bedroom...down the hall."

She sighed. "Fine."

Was this how they were going to be? Like two polite strangers under the same roof?

At least he was being cooperative about the whole thing. There'd been times when Chuck's resentment at being trapped was so palpable it flavored the air. Mandy had no intention of letting things go that far with Lucas. She'd tasted discontent. She had no intention of experiencing it again.

Lucas hadn't realized he had the jitters until he sat down at the table to eat pecan waffles. Mandy sat across the table exuding a sort of wary watchfulness, the children buzzed like bees with excitement over the horses, and Evelyn was knocking herself out to fill the awkwardness with welcome-to-our-family noises.

This is my family, Lucas said to himself, and suddenly the tightness in his chest dissolved. He leaned back in his chair and relaxed for the first time in months. There was an inevitableness to it all, a sense that at long last he no longer had to run.

That's what he'd been doing for years. Not chasing freedom on a GoldWing bike, but running for dear life. He was home now. Finally, he could breathe.

He smiled at his future mother-in-law. "These are the best pecan waffles I've ever tasted."

"I made them especially for you," Evelyn said.

Lucas felt like crying. Nobody ever made anything especially for him. His mother probably had, but his memory wouldn't stretch that far back. Long ago, he'd blocked most of his memories of the time before the fire. They'd been too painful for him. The loss had been too great for a small child to bear.

"Thank you, Evelyn. That's one of the nicest things anyone has ever done for me."

She got out of her chair to hug him. "Call me Mom," she said.

Over the top of her head, he could see Mandy's face. She looked as if she might cry, and as much as he didn't want that to happen, Lucas couldn't help but see her tears as a good sign.

"Everything's going to be all right," Evelyn whispered before she sat down, and he wondered at her reassurance for the thing that worried him most: the future of his children, the future of all of them.

"Is Lucas going to be our daddy?" Jill piped up.

"Eat your waffles, Jill," Mandy said, refusing to look at Lucas.

Jill was not to be sidetracked. "Is Lucas going to be our *daddy?*"

"We want him to, Mommy," Betsy said. "We voted."

"Who called this caucus?" Mandy's cheeks were flushed and her eyes bright.

"I did." Rusty stood up and puffed out his chest. "In the front yard. He brought us *horses.*"

"You don't decide this matter or any other matter that affects this family without me. All for one and one for all, remember?"

The entire discussion fascinated Lucas. There was love here. Lots of it. Nobody got mad and yelled. Nobody huffed off with hurt feelings. There was merely a healthy give and take between a mother who wasn't afraid to show fearless love and the children who loved her right back.

"All for one and one for all," the children chorused. Then Rusty said, "But what about the horses?"

Mandy gave Lucas a beseeching look. Such tenderness rose up in him that for a moment he couldn't speak.

Help me, Mandy mouthed.

"The horses are yours, no matter what." The children clapped and yelled, and Mandy rewarded him with one of her glorious smiles. For the moment, it was enough.

"Who wants to ride?" he added, and there was more happy hubbub from the children.

Then Rusty fell silent. "Wait a minute. I got to watch the Blue Angels on TV. My teacher said so. I gotta write a report."

In his single-minded pursuit of Mandy, Lucas had completely forgotten about the demonstration of the precision flight team from Pensecola Naval Air Station.

"Mind if I join you, Rusty?" he said. "The lieutenant commander is a friend of mine."

"You know the *Bear?*" Rusty looked at him with shining eyes, and Lucas grew two feet taller. He loved being a hero to this child. And if the fates were kind, he would never let him down. *Never.*

"Sure do. I was nearly grown when Jim Standing Bear came to the orphanage carrying his little brother, Ben. I'll never forget the look on his face. It's the same look he gets when he climbs into his plane, that nothing-can-defeat-me look." He held out his hand and Rusty grabbed ahold. "Come on, I'll show you."

Jill raced around the table and caught his britches, then held her arms up, smiling. "Me, too," she said.

"You bet, little angel." He scooped her up as well as Betsy, who was lagging behind, too shy to ask.

Mandy tried to hide the fact that she was wiping her eyes, but Lucas took note and exulted. Not that he would try to use her children. Not by a long shot. But there was something warm and reassuring about the children being in his corner.

"Coming, Mama?" Rusty said.

"I have to go to the bakery." Was that longing Lucas saw in her face, or was he simply projecting his own wishes? "Have a good time, and mind Grandma," she said, then she kissed all of her children, standing on tiptoe so she could reach Jill and Betsy.

Lucas didn't help her a bit. He could have leaned down or held both girls out for her, but he wanted Mandy to have to stand close to him. He wanted to feel her skin brush against his. He wanted to inhale the scent caught in her hair.

"Have a good day, Mandy," he told her as if it were something he said every day. "I'll see you this evening."

Knowing that he would was about the most wonderful thing he could think of. And that surprised Lucas. Wouldn't it be ironic to discover at the age of forty that he'd been running all his life from nothing but shadows?

Mandy hurried out of the kitchen, but not before Lucas said to Evelyn, "Come on, Mom. You get the seat of honor."

She tried to shoo them off. "Go ahead and have your fun. I'll do the dishes."

"We'll all do the dishes later. All for one and one for all," Lucas said, and he could tell by the stiffening of Mandy's back that she'd heard that, too.

Then she was out of sight, and he was settled into the midst of her family. *His* family.

Lucas was glad Evelyn had closed the shades and turned off the lamp so there wouldn't be a glare on the TV screen. It gave him a chance to blink away the moisture in his own eyes.

Later, he would teach Rusty that it was okay for grown men to cry. But not today. Not on Lucas's first day as a part of a family he could call his own.

Mandy cried so hard on her way to the bakery that she had to stop at the service station and wash her face. She didn't want to upset Josie and Myrtle, and she certainly didn't want to make a bad impression on Millicent on her first day.

The familiar misgivings plagued her. "Don't go there," she told herself, and then she parked her car and marched into her bakery as if she had the world by the tail.

She figured somebody should award her a trophy for best actress.

"Good morning, everyone," she said, smiling.

Today she would cope; tonight she would cry. It was the way of women.

Chapter Twenty-Three

His belongings were in her house, his feet under her table, and his horses stabled in her hometown. For all the good that did him, Lucas might as well still be in Arizona.

Mandy had been polite to him at dinner, cheerful even, and her mother and children treated him like a hero. Still, standing in the guest bedroom alone, Lucas felt the mantle of defeat settling over him.

Unless he did something fast he was going to be buried at another Wounded Knee.

Lucas turned his face to the breeze coming through his open window. A full moon was snagged in the treetops, and the stars were just beginning to appear. All was quiet in the house. He knew what he had to do.

Stealth was not his intention, and yet when he found her, Mandy was standing at her window, unaware. Was she thinking the same things he'd been thinking? Did the moon remind her of making love on a blanket of many colors? Did the stars make her heart beat faster?

She looked so small standing with her head against the windowpane, so vulnerable. Lucas stood in the doorway taking it all in.

Her covers were thrown back, her pillow mussed. She'd had trouble sleeping, too. He tried to drum up some satisfaction in that, but couldn't. Her shoulders were so narrow, her neck so slender. It wasn't right for her to carry the burden alone.

"I'll be the man of the house," she'd told Rusty.

Rusty had cornered Lucas that afternoon in the pecan grove for a man-to-man talk. After he'd told Lucas about his confrontation in the school yard and the subsequent conversation with his mother, he'd posed the question, "Are you gonna be the man of the house, now, 'cause my mama's 'bout got more than she can handle."

The boy had been deadly serious, and Lucas knew that nothing less than the truth would do. He wished he could tell Rusty that he would be the man of the house forever, but he was walking a thin line. He couldn't say anything that would put Mandy in a bad light with her son.

"I'll be the man of the house as long as your mother thinks that's the right thing for me to do."

The answer satisfied Rusty, and he'd made a quick transition back to a little boy.

"Reckon you can teach me a rope trick or two? Now that I got a horse, I'm plannin' on bein' a cowboy when I grow up."

So much was riding on Lucas. It was not only his future and Mandy's he had to consider, but the future of her children and her mother as well.

He sent a silent prayer winging toward the Great Spirit, a prayer for success, but most of all a prayer for wisdom.

"Mandy." She turned at the sound of his voice, and he could see that she'd been crying. Lucas stepped into her bedroom and shut the door. "Let me take your burden."

He held out his arms and she came to him, soft and sweet and smelling of roses.

"Oh, Lucas," she whispered, then leaned her head against his chest. He buried his face in her hair.

"Let me take care of you, Mandy."

She went still, and he waited. Finally she sighed, and he felt her body weight as she sagged against him.

"There is something you can do for me, Lucas."

"Anything, anything at all."

"Could you rub my back? This extra weight I'm carrying around has played havoc with it."

He picked her up and carried her to the bed.

"What are you doing? This is not an invitation for a romp on the playground."

He grinned. "Is that what you call your bed? A playground? I *like* that."

"You would. You were always lusty."

"I still am." He laid her on the bed, and when he leaned over her, her eyes widened.

"What are you planning to do, Lucas? Show me?"

"Only if you ask like a lady." He kissed her softly on the mouth. "But first, I'm going to rub your back."

"Don't know if I can trust you."

"I don't know if I trust me, either. Maybe you should chase me out with a broom, then lock the door."

He made her laugh, which was his intention all along. He didn't want to see Mandy in a state of anxiety, but more than that, he didn't want to be part of the cause.

She rolled onto her side, and he started the massage at her shoulders. She gave a deep sigh.

"I think I've found heaven," she said.

So have I, he thought, but, still leery of tempting the fates, he kept it to himself.

Mandy could almost believe that Lucas was her husband, that he'd pledged to love and cherish her forever. In her opinion, back rubs were right up there with hugging on the list of things that denoted cherishing.

Just as she'd begun to relax, Lucas said, "This would feel better if you were to take your top off."

She jerked straight up and pointed to the door. "Leave right now before I throw you out."

"What? What did I do?"

Oh, he was good all right. His innocent act was so convincing she almost bought it herself.

"You know perfectly well what I'm talking about."

"Mandy, I honestly don't have a clue."

"Well, then, let me spell it out for you. First, you weasel your way into my family, then you sneak in here under the guise of helping me."

His expression changed from puzzled to hurt. Almost, Mandy relented. Almost, Mandy believed in his good intentions. Once she got on a roll, though, it was hard to stop.

"Then you carry me off to bed like some prize you've won in a battle, and now you're…you're…" Suddenly she ran out of steam.

"Are you finished?"

"Just leave," she whispered.

"No."

"Please."

"I'll do anything you ask except that."

His eyes burned through her like blue-hot coals. If there was one thing she'd learned about Gray Wolf it was that he never took orders. *Never.* Why hadn't she already learned that?

"Lie down," he said.

"I will not."

"All right, then. Move over so I can finish what I started."

"I think you've done quite enough already."

"I came to this bed to give you a back rub, and that's what I'm going to do. Whether you like it or not."

They tried to stare each other down again, like two wild animals. *What have we come to?* she wondered. In the woods they'd been so perfect, and now they couldn't be in the same room without fighting.

Still, in spite of everything, she loved him, loved him with her entire being. She told him the only way she could, silently. *I love you, Lucas Gray Wolf.*

As if he'd read her thoughts, his face softened and he cupped her cheek.

"Mandy, whether you believe this or not, I *did* come here tonight to help you. You looked so tired at dinner I was worried about you."

Her resistance crumbled. How could she hold out against him when he was tender? How could she shut him out when his eyes turned the color of love and his heart was in his voice?

I love you, she thought. "I believe you," she said, and then she began to undo her buttons. She heard his sharp intake of breath, then looked up expecting to see desire. What she saw instead was such wonderment that her heart broke right in two.

How could a man look at a woman in that way, and yet not love her? How could he?

Say the words, she willed him. *Say the words and I'm yours.*

But he didn't. Instead he brushed aside her top, then cupped her heavy breasts and studied them as if they were rare treasures.

"You are so beautiful," he murmured. "More beautiful than I dreamed."

"You dream of me?"

"Every day and every night. Especially after I knew you carried my baby. I would ride up to the site where I'm building our house and spread my blankets under the stars and picture how you would look lying beside me, naked, your belly stretched with my child."

She was almost too full to speak. *Say it,* she pleaded silently. *Say you love me.*

She watched and waited while he massaged her cupped breasts with a reverence that stole her breath.

"Your children," she reminded him, when she could find her voice.

"Yes, my children." He kissed her softly on the lips. "Thank you, Mandy. You've given me the most beautiful gift in the world. You've given me a dream I never even knew I'd dreamed."

He'd done the same for her. The only difference was that she'd known her dreams. From the moment Gray Wolf followed her to her camp in the woods, she'd dreamed of lying with him, of loving him, of bearing his child. For in her opinion that was the ultimate gift of a woman for the man she loved, to bear his children.

She lay against the pillows and lifted her arms. "Come to me. Lie with me and be my Gray Wolf and I'll be your Lady."

"What about that massage? Don't you want it?"

"Yes...all over."

He hesitated, and she understood. "It's all right," she said. "You won't hurt me."

There was no guile in his Lady, no ulterior motives, only his Mandy looking up at him with the clear, green eyes that had lived in his dreams for the last few months, that would live in his dreams forever.

Warmth flooded his soul, and he bent over her as if she were rare porcelain. Supporting his body weight with his arms, he kissed her forehead, her cheek, her throat, her lips. The taste of her was both familiar and excitingly different, as if some exotic strain of flower had cross-pollinated with a cottage garden rose.

Starved for the taste of her, Lucas kissed until they were both panting for air. He gazed into her flushed face.

"I want to see you naked, Mandy. All of you."

"I'll show you." There was no hesitation in her, no coyness. As she had done that first night in the woods, when Mandy made up her mind to give herself to him, she gave one hundred percent.

She got off the bed and stripped, letting her clothes fall to the floor. Then she stood quietly while his eyes roamed over her. He couldn't get enough of looking. He marveled at the richness of her body, the fullness.

"Can I turn on the light?" he asked. "I want to see you more clearly."

She did it for him. Walking with the boldness and confidence of a goddess, she turned on the lamp, then moved in close enough so that he could touch.

He cupped her abdomen, splaying his hands across the creamy skin that was blue-veined and tight with his children. Ripples appeared underneath his hands, and he felt the hot sting of tears.

"They're moving," he whispered, awestruck.

"They recognize their daddy's voice."

"How?"

"I've told them."

He knelt and kissed her ripe belly, and then because he was overcome with an emotion he couldn't name, he kissed her swollen feet. She wove her hands in his hair and gently tugged him upward.

"There," she said, "there is where I want you to kiss me."

He buried his face in her, then felt her tremble, blossom, ripen at his touch. She moaned, and he braced her back with his hands while he continued an exploration that drove them both wild.

"I've missed this *so*," she said, her words coming out on spurts of ragged breath.

"So have I." He lifted her up and carried her to the bed. Levered over her, he made one last plea. "Please, don't let me hurt you."

"You won't. I promise."

His hunger fierce, his control almost shattered, he slowly slid into her. *Home,* he thought. *I am home.*

Filled with thanksgiving, he began a careful, quiet rhythm that shook him to the roots of his soul. Never before had he understood the power of tenderness.

"More," she whispered. "I want more." Lifting her hips, she thrust strongly against him, and he felt the heaviness of her belly.

"Wait." Lucas turned her on her side, then spooned against her.

"Perfect," she whispered, then sighing, she guided him home once more.

And there he stayed until the moon began to fade and the net of stars fell from the sky.

Chapter Twenty-Four

When Lucas woke up he was snuggled against Mandy spoon-fashion with his face in the warm soft curve of her neck. He lay still, listening. What woke him? A noise? A whisper? A dream?

Sighing, Mandy snuggled closer. Lucas tightened his grip lest someone snatch her away from him. Moving cautiously so as not to wake her, he shifted his weight to relieve the cramp in his leg.

And that's when he felt the lump under his pillow. No wonder he couldn't sleep. Easing his arm back, he reached under the pillow and pulled out two fat envelopes. In the half-light of approaching dawn, he saw that one contained the house plans, the other, the tickets to Italy.

The dreams he'd given her. She'd been sleeping with them under her pillow. He slipped the envelopes back into place, then fitted himself tightly to her and buried his face in her hair.

He would die before he'd ever lose this woman.

Lucas was sleeping flat on his back, one arm flung across his forehead, the other resting protectively over Mandy's belly. She lay perfectly still, luxuriating in his touch, exulting at finding herself awake with Lucas sharing her bed.

This is how it would be, she thought, and she knew she couldn't postpone the inevitable much longer. They were meant to be together, whether he thought so or not. She had her children to think about, too. They would only be confused if she continued the present situation.

Lucas Gray Wolf was *not* Chuck Belinda. Chuck had professed love, then made it a lie. Lucas had shown love, but refused to acknowledge it. She preferred the latter to the former.

Mandy sighed. Why couldn't she have it all? Was that too much to ask?

Probably. Very few people were lucky enough to have every one of their dreams come true.

She leaned on her elbow and studied him while he slept. His shoulders were wide, his arms beautifully muscled, his chest the stuff of every woman's secret desire. Just looking at him heated her blood.

Her quick passion amazed and thrilled her. She was so big she could hardly see her feet, and yet she'd never felt sexier, never felt more appealing, never felt more desirable.

Filled with wonder, Mandy reached out and caressed his chest. Lucas woke instantly, then lay perfectly still, his blue eyes piercing her.

"Good morning," he said. Then, when he reached for her, she gently pushed him back to the bed.

"Lie still. There's something I want to do first."

"What?"

"It's a surprise."

"Give me a hint. Is it a good something or a bad something?"

"Both," she whispered. Thus empowered, she bent over and took him in her mouth.

Lucas moaned. Fireworks exploded through him. Stars shot back into the sky. The moon and the sun collided. Heaven and earth were in turmoil, and he was caught at the vortex, spinning out of control.

Reality came to him in snatches, a glimpse of bright red hair, the curve of Mandy's belly, a long, lovely length of leg, the milk-ripe heaviness of her breasts. He was a rocket set to launch.

"Please," he groaned, and she lifted her face and smiled at him.

On fire, he reached for her, laid her back against the pillows and closed his mouth over a dark rosy nipple. She pulled him close, murmuring sweet encouragement, cradling his head, rocking him, loving him, and he suckled like a wild thing, starving.

"Lucas," she whispered. "Oh, Lucas." Then she pressed her arms close to her sides, lifting herself up for him. He moved from one breast to the other, a giant monarch, drunk on nectar.

Beneath him, she was silk and flame, slithering, burning, burning, until neither of them could endure the tiniest space of separation. She reached for him, guiding him into that rich, welcoming warmth where lay all the treasures of the world.

Braced, Gray Wolf made sweet hot love to his Lady

until the clock on her bedside table announced the start of another day.

"I wish this could go on forever," she whispered.

So did he, but he didn't dare tell her so. Instead, he brought them both to a soft, screaming satisfaction, then spilled his seed.

Where it belongs, he thought. But he didn't say that either.

Quietly, he gathered his clothes and left the room while she lay naked and flushed on her bed.

It was Sunday morning. Soon the children would be stirring and he was still only a guest.

Her mother was already in the kitchen when Mandy got downstairs. Evelyn poured herself a cup of coffee, then got a glass of milk for Mandy and sat down at the kitchen table.

"The moonflowers are still in bloom," she said.

"I know that." Mandy reached for her milk while Evelyn pursed her lips and gave one of her famous looks.

"Just wanted to remind you, that's all."

"Is there a point to this conversation, Mother?"

"I'm not going to beat around the bush. A quiet family wedding in the gazebo would be beautiful. We wouldn't have to spend a penny on flowers."

"I'm not marrying again just because I'm pregnant." Mandy didn't even sound convincing to herself. She doubted very seriously if she'd fooled her mother.

"A man like Lucas Gray Wolf comes along only once in a lifetime, and that's all I'm saying on the subject."

"Good."

"Unless I change my mind."

Mandy smiled. She couldn't help herself. This morning

she felt good all over. Why pretend to be a hard-nosed woman?

Lucas came into the kitchen, his hair still wet from the shower, and Mandy's smile moved straight to his heart.

"Good morning," she said, as if she'd only just set eyes on him.

"It is, isn't it?" His smile warmed her to her toes. She was still tingling when he turned his attention to her mother. "Morning, Mom. Got any of that coffee left?"

"I saved the best cup for you." Evelyn gave Mandy an arch look, then sashayed to the pot and poured Lucas a cup, making a big to do of it. She probably would have put on an equally dramatic show coming back to the table, but the telephone interrupted her act.

"It's for you, Lucas." Mandy handed him the phone. "Steve Thunderhorse."

"What's up, pal?" Concern crossed Lucas's face, and then absolute joy.

"He has a son," Lucas told them, after he'd hung up. "It came early, but Angel and the baby are both fine."

Selfish terror gripped Mandy. "You'll be going home, then?"

"I arranged for extra help on the ranch before I came here." He looked straight into her eyes. "I *am* home, Mandy."

Evelyn gave her daughter an I-told-you-so look, then emptied Lucas's cup and refilled it with hot coffee.

"I was thinking a Sunday picnic would be nice," she said, sitting down beside him. "Just us family."

It was Lucas's first Southern-style picnic. They went to Lake Lamar Bruce, where Evelyn spread two patchwork quilts Mandy's grandmother made, and laid out a sumptuous banquet that included fried chicken, potato salad, pecan pies and an array of casseroles Lucas couldn't pretend to name. Every bit of it was delicious.

He reached for another piece of chicken. "I'm afraid I'm making a pig of myself."

"I'd be disappointed if you didn't," Evelyn remarked, beaming at him. "That's the best compliment a cook can have."

The children had long since lost interest in the food and were climbing trees and playing chase at the water's edge. Mandy was reclining against the trunk of a huge magnolia, legs outstretched, feet crossed at the ankles, looking as serene as a Boticelli painting of the Madonna.

Lucas smiled at her over the top of his chicken, and she gave him that radiant, transforming smile that never ceased to render him awestruck. He had found paradise.

A loud scream shattered the peace. Rusty raced toward them, yelling, "Betsy's in the water."

The first scream set Lucas in motion, up and running toward the lake. The second froze his blood. It came from behind him…and it came from Mandy.

Over his shoulder he saw her fall, her arms spread out like wings. Evelyn raced to her fallen daughter. "Get Betsy," she yelled. "Go on! Hurry!"

Mandy lay on the ground, unmoving, one leg twisted, her arms wrapped protectively around her belly. Lucas stopped breathing. For an instant he hung suspended between two kinds of hell, then he continued his race to the water.

With a sister in the water and their mother down on the ground, Jill and Rusty went wild with screaming. Lucas saw the little body, bobbing like a cork.

His agony found no voice. Some screams happen on the inside.

She disappeared then popped back up, her little hands

flailing. Thanking the Great Spirit, Lucas swam out and grabbed her just as she was going under again.

She clung to his neck, sputtering and coughing.

"Are you okay, Betsy?"

"I'm mad, that's all. If that tree limb hadn't broke I wouldn'ta fell in that ole water." She coughed again. "It glugged and glugged me."

Evelyn met them at the water's edge and wrapped Betsy in one of the quilts. Mandy was still on the ground.

"Is she...?"

"She's not bleeding, thank God. I'm..."

The rest of what she said was lost as Lucas Gray Wolf ran toward his Lady. The distance between them stretched as endless as the Sahara, and in the time it took for him to go from lake's edge to the spot where she'd fallen, he shook the heavens with his pleas.

Let her live and I'll never leave her side again.

Let the babies live and I'll be the best father on earth.

Don't take my family from me. Please, God.

"Mandy..." He knelt beside her, cradling her face with his hands. "Don't die, Mandy. Don't leave me."

She was bleached of all color, white as bones, her eyelashes like soot against her skin. Her eyes fluttered open, and she tried a smile that turned into a grimace.

"I won't leave you, Lucas. Now or ever." She touched his face, her fingertips cool as mountain springs. "Don't you know...? I love you."

The whine of the siren became louder as the ambulance hove into view. "I called with the cell phone," Evelyn said.

Too full to speak, Lucas held Mandy's hand, held on so tightly he meant never to let go. Voices came to him through a fog calling out blood pressure, heart rate, instructions to one another as the paramedics gingerly lifted her onto the gurney.

Still he held on, afraid to let go, terrified of losing her.

Evelyn touched his arm. "Betsy's okay. I'll take the children in the car. You go with Mandy in the ambulance."

He nodded, blindly holding onto the woman who was more than life itself to him. Cramped in the small space with his blood roaring as loudly as the siren, Lucas could see only one thing, Mandy's face. He could hear only one voice, the echo of her whispering, *Don't you know...? I love you.*

Love for her overwhelmed him, took away his sanity, his breath, his voice. All these months he'd denied his feelings, afraid of tempting the fates, afraid of losing her the same way he'd lost everything in his life he'd ever loved.

And in one careless moment he'd almost lost her anyway. It was another of life's lessons, another of life's huge ironies.

Forgive me for being a slow student, he silently prayed.

He bent close to her, smoothed her hair back from her forehead. "Mandy, I..."

Her groan interrupted him, and Lucas had to stand aside while the medics worked over her.

The hospital loomed, tires squealed, the siren shut down and Mandy was whisked away from him. Too tense to sit, Lucas leaned against the wall, waiting. Evelyn and the children joined him. She thrust a cup of black coffee into his hands.

"Mandy's a strong fighter," she said, "and so are all my grandchildren, including those babies." She patted his hand. "We're going to get through this together."

He'd never been more grateful for family. They were a buffer against the strong winds of adversity, a shield against threatening missiles, a bunker of safety in the midst of attack.

A small eternity later, the doctor joined them. "She's going to be all right. Nothing more than a sprained ankle."

Lucas's blood began to flow once more. His heart started beating again. He could breathe.

He sent silent prayers of thanksgiving winging upward. Mandy had been returned to him, a gift to love. Was it too much to ask that his babies be, as well? He was almost afraid to ask.

"The babies?" he said.

"As far as we can tell, everything is all right." It was incredible after such a fall. A miracle. "We've seen falls like this before," the doctor said, as if he'd read Lucas's thoughts. "The protective instincts of the mother, combined with the protective qualities of the womb usually come into play in cases like this."

He clapped Lucas on the shoulder. "You're a very lucky man."

"The luckiest man alive."

He looked at Evelyn, and she smiled at him. "Go on in and see her. We'll wait."

The color had returned to Mandy's face, but she looked so fragile lying against the white sheets that Lucas was almost afraid to touch her.

"Hey, you," she said, lifting her arms. "Come here."

He wrapped her close to his heart and buried his face in her hair.

"I thought I'd lost you, Mandy."

"I'm here. And so are the babies."

He inhaled her scent, reveled in the touch of her silky

hair, exulted in the feel of holding her in his arms once more. She gave him a good, strong squeeze.

"I'm not that easy to get rid of, you know," she whispered, and Lucas lifted his head to look into her dear face. He wanted to memorize her, every inch of her so that when she was away from him, even for a second, he could delve into his storehouse of memories and see her as clearly as if she were in his arms.

"There's something I have to tell you, Mandy. Something I should have told you a long time ago."

She was still, waiting and watching him with eyes as bright as neon. He stroked her cheeks, traced her eyebrows, her nose, her lips.

"I love you," he whispered. "I love every inch of you. I always have and I always will."

She stared at him for such a long time that he got scared. Had he waited too late? Was she going to say, "Thanks," then try to send him packing?

Those shining eyes bore into him as he waited for her answer. She'd said she loved him, too, but maybe she was tired of waiting. Maybe she wanted more.

"I want to be your Gray Wolf and I want you to be my Lady. Now and forever," he said.

"Yes," she whispered. "Oh, yes."

A week later, Mandy and Lucas were married in the gazebo in the pecan grove with the entire family looking on and moonflowers scenting the air. While a moon as big as a galleon rode the sky, Lucas danced by turn, first with Evelyn, then Betsy and Jill while Rusty, looking important in the tuxedo that matched his new daddy's, manned the tape machine.

"I've saved the best for last," Lucas whispered when he finally took Mandy in his arms.

As they twirled to the strain of "I'll Never Stop Loving You," the family quietly vanished and the stars popped into the heavens, one by one.

"Remember that evening I gave you the stars," she whispered.

"Always."

"I'm going to give them to you again."

"You already have. Every moment I spend with you is a moment filled with stars."

Smiling, she stepped back and unbuttoned her dress, and there shining across her stomach and trailing downward were the paste-on stars.

Lucas knelt in front of her and kissed them off one by one, starting where his babies' hearts beat strong and proud, and ending with Venus.

The goddess of love.

Epilogue

In June, when the willow trees dipped green limbs into the Verde River and colts gamboled in the pastures at Paradise Ranch to the delight of three children who hung on the fence, nannies kept watch over two strong, happy babies. Evelyn reigned supreme in the glass and stone house that overlooked it all, and Lucas Gray Wolf had taken his Lady on a belated honeymoon to Venice.

There on a bed with ivory-colored satin sheets he rediscovered the stars. French doors were flung open to the breeze and outside, the cypress trees danced. Church bells called worshipers to evening prayers and doves lifted toward the setting sun on snow-white wings.

Mandy had let her hair grow long, and it fanned across the sheets like flame. Lucas lifted the silky strands so they caught the light of the fading sun, then let them filter through his fingers.

"I could spend all night just admiring your hair," he said.

"I have a few other things in mind for this honeymoon," she said, and then she showed him.

Her body was lush, her breasts full. She raised herself to her knees and offered them up to Lucas like a chalice. He took the nipples engorged with childbirth and love into his mouth, and gently suckled where his son and his daughter had so recently nestled.

She cradled his head, murmuring, "I love you, Lucas Gray Wolf. I love you." And when her love words become incoherent with passion, he lowered her to the sheets and thrust home.

She wrapped her arms around him, and he began a slow, leisurely journey that gradually escalated to a heart-pounding, blood-roaring passage to the stars. As they lay tangled on the sheets limp and sated, he planted a long, lingering kiss on his wife's lips.

"Now, Mrs. Gray Wolf, love of my life, heart of my heart, is there anything else I can do for you?"

"There's just one little thing." She lifted herself on her elbow and gazed down at him, eyes shining.

"I'd do anything in the world for you, give you anything you desire." He cupped her face and kissed her again. "Especially when you look at me like that. Now, tell me, what is this thing?"

"Don't you even want to know if it's a good thing or a bad thing?" she asked, teasing him.

"Lady, with you it's always both."

She laughed, then to show he was right, she blazed a trail of hot kisses from his throat to his groin.

He pulled her against him and held her so close he could feel her heart beating to the same rhythm as his.

"I take it you're in no rush to do this new thing." His

voice was hoarse, and his body was making a remarkable comeback.

"Hmm," she murmured. "Not necessarily."

"Would sometime within the next few centuries be all right?" He slid into her soft welcoming folds.

"Definitely."

Much, much later she told him what she wanted. The next evening Lucas made Mandy's dream come true. While she reclined and gazed up at the stars he guided the gondola he'd rented to a secluded spot in the canals. Then, weighing anchor, he covered her with his blanket and there under the rainbow of colors where they lay joined soul to soul, heart to heart, Lucas Gray Wolf sang Sioux love songs in his native tongue and pledged his love to his Lady.

For all time.

* * * * *

SILHOUETTE®
SPECIAL EDITION™

AVAILABLE FROM 21ST JUNE 2002

DADDY IN DEMAND Muriel Jensen

That's My Baby!

When Dori McKeon found an abandoned baby she turned to estranged husband Sal Dominguez. Sal was happy to help solve the puzzle—and to try and win Dori back...this time—forever!

THE STRANGER IN ROOM 205 Gina Wilkins

Hot Off the Press

Instinct told newspaper owner Serena Schaffer that the injured man she'd found was not who he proclaimed to be. But one look into Sam's eyes and Serena was ready to believe anything...

WHEN I SEE YOUR FACE Laurie Paige

Windraven Legacy

Rory Daniels knew that if temporarily blinded Shannon Bannock could just find the courage to trust him, he could show her so much—he could show her forever...

STORMING WHITEHORN Christine Scott

Montana Brides

Storm Hunter had coldly refused Jasmine's charms. The chasm between their ages and cultures was too wide. But how could Storm continue to resist when the virginal beauty still looked at him that way?

STARTING WITH A KISS Barbara McMahon

When prim-and-proper Abigail Trent asked Dr Greg Hastings to help turn her into an irresistible temptress, she never thought that after just one kiss she would start to hope that Greg was her Prince Charming...

STRANGER IN A SMALL TOWN Ann Roth

B&B owner and single mum Alison O'Hara was like no woman loner Clint had ever met. Could she transform him into a husband—and a daddy to her little girl?

0602/23a

AVAILABLE FROM 21ST JUNE 2002

SILHOUETTE®

Sensation™

Passionate, dramatic, thrilling romances

FUGITIVE HEARTS Ingrid Weaver
THE SEDUCTION OF GOODY TWO-SHOES Kathleen Creighton
THE SHERIFF'S SURRENDER Marilyn Pappano
BORN A HERO Paula Detmer Riggs
PROTECTOR WITH A PAST Harper Allen
MOONGLOW, TEXAS Mary McBride

Intrigue™

Danger, deception and suspense

NIGHT-TIME GUARDIAN Amanda Stevens
TO PROTECT THEIR CHILD Sheryl Lynn
SOMEONE TO PROTECT HER Patricia Rosemoor
THE ARMS OF THE LAW Jenna Ryan

Superromance™

*Enjoy the drama, explore the emotions,
experience the relationship*

WHITE PICKET FENCES Tara Taylor Quinn
THE NEGOTIATOR Kay David
A SELF-MADE MAN Kathleen O'Brien
SNOW BABY Brenda Novak

Desire™

Two intense, sensual love stories in one volume

HIS KIND OF WOMAN
THE TEXAN'S TINY SECRET Peggy Moreland
THE BARONS OF TEXAS: JILL Fayrene Preston

UP CLOSE AND PASSIONATE
LAST VIRGIN IN CALIFORNIA Maureen Child
UNDERCOVER SULTAN Alexandra Sellers

AND BABY MAKES THREE
HAVING HIS CHILD Amy J Fetzer
MIXING BUSINESS...WITH BABY Diana Whitney

0602/23b

THE STANISLASKI
Sisters

NORA ROBERTS

From the bestselling author of the Stanislaski Brothers, Nora Roberts brings you the spirited, sexy Stanislaksi Sisters.

Bestselling author of Night Tales

Available from 19th July 2002

Available at most branches of WH Smith, Tesco, Martins, Borders, Eason, Sainsbury's and most good paperback bookshops.

0802/121/SH30